The Cosmic Turkey

The Cosmic Turkey

Laura Ruth Loomis

Thinklings Books, LLC
Wickliffe, OH

1

A Town Not Called Martian

Thanks to recent advances in technology, my floatcar can self-navigate, adjust for traffic, and insult my outfit—but it still can't find me a decent parking space. If it could, I might have avoided the arrest that started the whole mess.

I was living in a town with no name, which sounds like it should be somewhere exotic and frontier-ish, but it was in Connecticut instead. I'd left high school three months early, after causing a slight accident in science class that turned the teacher into a giant electromagnet. He convinced the school to give me a diploma if I promised never to come back. I seemed to have a strange effect on anything mechanical, to the point where my ex-boyfriend Pietro called me Jam-it instead of Janet.

The town was only nameless because the corporation that had previously owned the naming rights, Interglobal Monotonous Generalities Unlimited, had gone bankrupt. According to the charter, we couldn't get a new name until the City Council had properly considered all suggestions, subjected them to public inquiry, and chosen the top seventeen for a vote. Tonight was the decision, and I was rooting for something meaningful, like Nerthus, the name of an ancient Scandinavian earth goddess. Or maybe something fun to say, like "Flibber-tigibbet." If nothing else, I was going to oppose names like Willow Springs for a town with no willows and no springs, or anything drab like Industry or Harmony or Saint Anything. I had vague plans to attend the local college, which would share the town's name, and Industry College sounded painfully dull.

I pulled my floatcar into the parking structure across from a brick building with a makeshift sign: "_____ City Hall." The garage was surprisingly compact, with vehicles stacked in columns of twenty, each hovering a few inches above the next. The whole place smelled like fuelstone, a nose-assaulting combination of burnt rubber and mildew. I passed up three different spaces that were a little too small, then got cut off for the next one by a Saturnian driving a Saturn. Finally, I squeezed into a spot in the top row.

My floatcar was one of the junky old ones, shaped like two criss-crossed canoes with eight antennas pointing out of random junctures. I couldn't help comparing it with the sleek model below, the kind that folded down to the size of a dinner plate. I couldn't afford the compact model, much less the fancy kind with the built-in time warp, where the pilot could send it into the future until it was needed. Those last ones were technically illegal, but rich people found ways to get around that, usually by paying the fine in some other century.

The meeting had overflowed from City Hall, so loudspeakers were set up in the courtyard and street in front of the building. I elbowed my way through the crowd in the courtyard: big-eyed Mercurians with their cone-shaped ears, tentacled Uranians, Venusians glowing with their mysterious inner light. And I, Janet Delane, one undersized human, squeezing my way between two gigantic Alpha Centaurians as I inched closer to the building.

A giant screen atop the building showed the scene inside: a human in a kiwi-colored suit and bow tie standing at the microphone. "I think we should call it Industry City."

"Boring," I muttered. "Do we even have any industries?" I worked at the only factory in town, a packing plant that made edible air.

A Venusian with a bright purple aura was entering the building. I couldn't tell from here if it was my ex-boyfriend Pietro, but it looked like his aura color. I decided I'd stay outside and watch the screen.

The next speaker was some sort of giant insect, possibly a mutated aphid, wearing a backward baseball cap. "Every town should have a good theme song," the bug said in a raspy voice like fingernails on plasteel. "Who doesn't love to hear *Chicago Is My Kind of Town,* or *I Left My Heart in San Francisco?* Or *It's Great to Be Alive in Death Valley?* So I've narrowed the name choices down to either *Unchained Melody* or *Your Love Is Like a Cold Slice of Pizza.* Or if you like country music, maybe *I'm Just a Bug on the Windshield of Life.*"

"Thank you," said the mayor, a helmet-haired Earthling descended from a long line of senators, governors, and upscale mobsters. She handed off the microphone to an elderly woman in a too-short okapi-print dress with *Zhorb* printed across the butt.

"Saint Zhorb doesn't have a single town named after him yet." The woman sounded outraged at the injustice.

"No saints," I groaned, trying to get around the shuttlecraft-sized Alpha Centaurian in front of me. "Would you want to see that on the side of a garbage truck? Saint Somebody trash removal?"

On my left, another gigantic Alpha Centaurian peered down and asked, "What religion is Saint Zhorb? Catholic or Flubertarian?"

"No idea!" I yelled back, hoping he could hear me up there.

A third Alpha Centaurian moved in on my right, so now I was completely wedged in. On the plus side, they radiated cold, which was a relief from the heat of the crowd. On the downside, they were blocking my view of the screen.

Voices kept booming from the loudspeakers. "Let's call it Glzrx-plexis!"

"I heard Queelchu will make a large donation if someone names a town after her."

"Queelchu? The actress? She hasn't made a holofilm in fifty years!"

"How about New New York?"

"There's already a New New York and an Old New York and a Middle-Aged York."

A familiar voice broke through. "We should name it Martian." I recognized the voice: it belonged to my brother, the only person who'd come up with that.

"This isn't Mars! It's Earth!" The gurgling voice told me a

Plutonian was speaking. Weren't we still at war with Pluto? It was hard to keep track.

"It's a great name," the first voice persisted. Definitely my brother. What was he doing here?

"How about New Mars?"

"Not Mars. Martian."

The Alpha Centaurian looked down at me again, his indigo eye larger than my head. "There are no Martians. Are there?"

"No!" I yelled back.

"What?" The Alpha Centaurian bent closer to hear me better. A lock of his hair flopped loose and knocked me over. "Sorry," he said, and reached a finger down to help me up.

From where I'd landed, sprawled on the ground facing away from the building, I was probably the only one who saw what happened next. A time-warped shuttlecraft blinked into existence near the top row of the parking structure. Someone must have set the timer wrong (underestimating the length of the meeting, no doubt). The time-warped craft displaced one of the fold-up models, which was jolted into unfolding, which in turn knocked another floatcar loose and sent it flying...straight across the street, through the screen, and into the roof of City Hall. Outlined in black was a giant smoking hole shaped like two crisscrossed canoes. A stray antenna dangled a pair of fuzzy twenty-sided dice, the ones I'd hung from my mirror for luck.

Unfortunately, my registration papers inside were still perfectly legible. I learned this when the speakers boomed, "Janet Delane, report to security!"

I contemplated trying to disappear, running off to Regulus Prime or something. But I'm even worse at rule breaking than I am at technology, and I couldn't bring myself to leave the scene of the crime. With assorted eyes and eyestalks staring at me, I made my way inside to the security desk, which was staffed by a four-inch-tall Betelgeusian. There was a twisted glowing paperweight next to the desk, which I eventually realized was the remains of my floatcar.

I tried to explain my situation to the security officer. "It wasn't my fault. It got hit by the time-warp shuttlecraft that reappeared."

"There was no time-warp craft found in the parking structure." He didn't even look up from the papers on his desk, probably because it took all his strength and concentration to handle a pen that was as tall as he was.

"It must have time-warped out of there," I argued.

He gave a tiny snort. "That's what they all say."

"So this has happened before?"

The Betelgeusian finished writing out my citation, then laboriously tore it off of the pad and held it up to me. It looked like a tarp over his head. Who even uses real pens and paper anymore, instead of plasma slates?

"You're to report tomorrow to the Superior Court of the City of..." He called out to the people who were still milling around, "Did we ever decide on a name for this burg?"

"New Saint Harmony York Springs," answered a bright green Saturnian.

"Ugh." I rubbed my temples.

"Yeah," the Betelgeusian said, "I was hoping for Glzrxplexis."

The next day, I went to plead my case before the court. A makeshift banner with the town's new name drooped across the courtroom wall, partially obscuring a portrait of the mayor with her pet emu. Half the letters were obscured in the folds, so it looked like it said "Newt Hark...rings."

A violet glow alerted me to Pietro's presence in the corner. He snapped a picture, then started typing furiously on his phone, probably posting on his blog. I made a point of ignoring him and watching the trials before mine. Pietro snickered, just loud enough for me to hear.

The other defendants included people charged with petty theft, defacing corporate logos, ballroom dancing under the influence of hallucinogenic quarks, and sneaking candy into a movie theater. I was surprised by that last one: who knew our town had a movie theater?

Some offenders got off with fines, one was accidentally acquitted, and a few were led away to jail. The jail uniforms were a cheerful yellow, with an ad on the back for a children's breakfast cereal.

When my turn came, the robot judge was unimpressed with my explanation. "The damage to the building was forty-four million credits," it intoned metallically. We have the technology to give robots human voices, so I assume it just liked sounding sinister. "You will reimburse the cost to the city."

I didn't have forty-four million credits. I probably didn't have four credits. "What about the time-warp vehicle?"

"There is no record of a time-warp vehicle being present on that occasion."

My voice rose in frustration. "Because it time-warped away!"

"That is what they all say. The court's decision is final. As a first offender, if you cannot pay the fine, you have a choice of one year in jail, one year in the military, or one year in GUPPEAS."

"Guppies?"

"The Galactic Universal Peacemongering Paradigm Emergent Action Spacefleet. A new project in interplanetary cooperation."

I'd never heard of it, but "peacemongering" sounded good. Jail sounded bad. Military sounded worse. So, GUPPEAS it would be. I was given thirty-seven-and-a-half hours to settle my affairs before reporting for duty.

There wasn't much to settle. I wouldn't miss my tedious job at the edible air factory, and they wouldn't miss me after I emailed my resignation. College might as well wait, since I had no idea what to study. As for dating, I'd given it up after Pietro dumped me the night of the zero-gravity prom, when he decided that little malfunction was my fault.

No school, no job to speak of, and no boyfriend. My parents were on assignment in another star system, and I'd have to send them a message explaining what had happened. Later, I decided. Right now, the only thing left to do was call my brother. I pulled out my GeniusPhone, which was last year's model but still had a higher IQ than the ex-boyfriend. Calling me Jam-it the Technology-Slayer, as if that even made sense! "GeniusPhone," I said, "place a call to—"

The phone sprayed a shower of red and green sparks, then gave a dramatic wheeze and fell apart in my hand.

I made the call from the call panel in the courthouse.

My brother's round face filled the screen, squinting as if he'd been out all night. "Hey, Janet."

A Uranian mer-slug came up behind me, dragging its tentacles and leaving a trail of goop on the floor. It pointed a tentacle at the call panel.

"Hi, I wanted to tell you—" I stopped. "Why are you bald?"

"I've been working on designing a hands-free razor, and it worked so well, I got a little carried away." My brother grinned. "Were you at the town hall meeting last night? It was wild."

The Uranian tapped a tentacle impatiently. Sorry, but I got the call panel first. "Was I there? Hello, my floatcar got knocked through the roof, and I was arrested!"

"Oh yeah—I forgot about that after the fight broke out between the Larch Springs people and the Saint Something-or-other people. And I had the best name."

"Martian—"

"Yeah, Martian. There isn't a single town on Earth named Martian."

"Martian, I have to tell you—"

The Uranian peered over my shoulder. "That's not a Martian," it said. "That's an Earthling."

My brother had this conversation often. "No, I'm Martian," he said.

"Everyone knows there's no such thing as Martians."

Usually I let him go on and confuse people if he felt like it. Not today. "His name is Martian. Martian Delane."

"But I was actually born on Saturn," he added helpfully.

"Not now!" I snapped. Once he got started on that story, there would be no dragging him back. "Martian, the reason I called is I got arrested, and they're making me join this thing called GUPPEAS. Peacemongering something something spacefleet. I need you to store some of my things."

"Can I use the parts from your floatcar?" Knowing Martian, he'd probably rejigger it into a musical toothbrush or a solar-powered Geiger-counting deep fryer.

"Sure, whatever's left of it."

"What did Mom and Dad say about the whole arrest thing?"

My face warmed with embarrassment. "I haven't told them yet. I'll figure something out."

"Cool. Let me know how to reach you."

"Thanks, Martian."

A Venusian walked by, giving off a translucent lavender glow. "That's not a Martian."

"Don't," I said. "Just don't."

The next day, I reported to the GUPPEAS headquarters with a duffel bag stuffed full of my belongings slung over my shoulder. I was greeted by a smirking Venusian man with slicked-back blue hair and a lime-green aura. I've heard that Venusians don't have auras on their home planet; it's some sort of reaction to the colder temperatures in the rest of the galaxy. Colors are very individual; my ex-boyfriend Pietro used to go from lavender to deep indigo to show degrees of pleasure. On the GUPPEAS officer, lime green apparently meant smarmy. His cologne had that new-spaceship smell, hot metal and glue, but his smile was more like a used-spaceship salesman.

"Janet Delane? Welcome to GUPPEAS. I'm Vertin Bogler, the Undersecretary to the Oversecretary to the Director of Recruitment and Retention." He handed me something that looked like an over-sized cell phone with straps at both ends. "Here's your beepity-beeper."

"My what?"

"Communications device. It's short for Boron-Edged Electrum-Powered Integrated Technological Yadayada Bifurcated Electronic Eleventy-Purpose Existential Radio."

"Of course it is. What else would it be short for?" I let him attach it to my arm with the straps.

"You don't get a weapon, of course, this being a peace organization." He gestured toward a device mounted on the wall. "We tried using felicinators, which put the targeted creature in a really good mood, but some species like Plutonians tend to torture people when they're in a good mood."

"Ah."

"Felicinator is short for…"

I stopped listening, his voice providing a dull background buzz as I looked out the office window at the spaceport. The ships hailed from all over the galaxy, and I recognized some of the styles, from the deceptively simple Saturnian saucers to the constantly moving Cassiopeian ships made of living matter. My eyes were drawn to one elegant ship that looked like a Terran design, shaped like a golden dragon with wings half unfurled. Would I get to serve on a ship like that?

"Captain Delane?" Bogler's voice broke in.

That was weird. There was a captain with my name?

Bogler took a heavy box off his desk, grunted, and thrust it into my arms. "Here are the forms you'll have to fill out." He picked up a pile of folded clothes in several too-bright colors, and tossed them on top of the box. "And there's your captain's uniform. I'll show you to your ship."

Wait, did he just call me "Captain"?

He flitted across the room to the lift, and I staggered after him as best as I could, half carrying and half dragging the box. "There must be some mistake. I'm not a captain; I'm a felon. The charge was wanton and mildly atrocious destruction of government property."

"That's all very interesting, Captain," he said. "But we never make that sort of mistake. Don't forget to get your paperwork done."

"Paper? You mean, like, from dead trees? Doesn't the ship's computer do your forms?"

"The forms aren't compatible with your ship's computer. We're not sure what *is* compatible with your ship's computer. We've sent it to seven technicians, a psychiatrist, and an acupuncturist."

We stepped off the lift and emerged next to the port, in an area that appeared to be the salvage yard. In front of us stood a battered husk of metal shaped like an ugly long-necked bird—a turkey, maybe—with the tail about to fall off. It was burned in some spots and rusted in others, with a shuttlecraft-sized hole in one side.

"Here's your ship," he said, giving it a cheerful pat.

I stared. "Can I change my mind and go to jail instead?"

The tail fell off.

2

Common Science Fiction Plot Devices

The ship looked worse on the inside. Wires and bolts jutted out in odd places, held together with paper clips, macramé, and something that resembled hollandaise sauce. I stood just inside the hatch and tried to orient myself. Voices drifted from somewhere down the passage ahead.

My crew. The thought made my throat go dry. How was I supposed to act like a real captain? I was fresh out of high school and had barely held a job.

They didn't know that, I reminded myself. If I carried myself with authority, maybe I could make a good first impression. I took a deep breath and headed down the cramped hallway, stopping to adjust my grip on the box of forms before making a dignified entrance onto the bridge.

The box slipped through my fingers and crashed to the floor, causing the whole ship to shudder.

The bridge was smaller than I'd expected—the size of my living room—with computer panels along the walls and a giant viewscreen in the front. There were stools at various stations. A bored-looking Venusian woman looked me up and down but didn't bother to comment on my presence as she fiddled with the blinking lights on the arm of a large captain's chair in the center.

My chair. Which she was currently occupying.

A crew member's legs extended from a hatch in the ceiling, where they were trying to weld the ship's tail back on. A puff of smoke circled lazily down from the hole.

"Hand me the portable blast container," came his voice from somewhere in the kidneys of the ship.

"We don't have one," the Venusian woman replied. Her aura was pink, and extended for a good six inches beyond her skin. She had reddish-blonde curls, a golden cast to her skin, a face like the statue of a goddess, and a scowl that could stun laserfish at ten paces.

"Well, give me something!" the man called. "Duct tape. Sandbags. An origami crane. Anything to stuff in this hole before the ship falls apart."

The woman tore open my box and handed an armload of forms up to him, followed by a scary-large blowtorch, then sat back down.

"Why is it always the tail?" squeaked a second voice from inside the hole. I couldn't tell who was speaking.

A curly-haired Mercurian man wandered into the room, looking dazed. Or maybe that was just his normal look, with his trumpet-shaped ears and overlarge eyes like two eggs sunny-side up.

"Um, hello," I said. The Mercurian glanced my way. The Venusian woman turned her attention to the computer, which seemed to be settling down.

"Attention!" I said, louder than I'd meant to. "Um, please."

The crewman in the hatch stuck his head out. He was covered in grime, but I could make out bright orange eyes and green hair like shredded lettuce. "Hello?"

"I'm Janet Delane. Your new captain."

The Venusian woman groaned. The Mercurian said, "Another one?"

Something resembling a three-foot-wide purple rubber ball bounced out of the hatch and settled next to me.

"How old are you?" the Venusian woman asked. Her voice had the exact tone of authority that mine didn't, and it made me want to scuttle for the exit.

"Eighteen. I think this assignment may be some sort of mistake," I said hopefully.

"That's what the last captain said," the Mercurian answered, smiling, "right before she took the shuttle and crashed it through the bulkhead and flew away."

"Shut up, Zeeko," said the other two. There might have been a third voice in there somewhere.

Mentally, I tried to regroup. What would a real captain do? I strode over to the captain's chair and stood over the Venusian woman, but she didn't budge. The words *You're in my chair* stuck in my throat.

I backed up, reached into the box, and pulled a form out at random. It said *Crew Manifest.* "So, who are you all?"

"I'm Frink," the grimy man said, "the pilot." He gave a last name, but it was something Ursa Majoran and unpronounceable, so I just wrote down, "Frink."

The purple ball sprouted two stubby legs.

The Venusian woman said, "Lolagnya og de Thurwolliger. First officer."

Should I ask her to spell it for me? She was still glowering. I wrote down, "Lola."

The purple ball sprouted eyes and a mouth, and said, "I'm Nlubglub," in the squeaky voice I'd heard earlier. "Security chief." I shouldn't have been surprised to realize the ball was a Jupiteran. A lot of Jupiterans were working in security these days, as their mutable forms made them impervious to most types of attack.

"How do you spell that?"

"Just like it sounds. N-L-U-B-G-L-U-B."

The Mercurian stood smiling obliviously.

"And you are?" I prompted.

"Zeeko."

"Spell that?"

"P-L-U-T-H-E-R-X-I-B."

Lola turned her scowl on him. "You don't know how to spell your own name?"

I wrote down "Zeeko," and asked, "What's your job?"

He thought carefully before answering. "I don't know."

"He just showed up one day," Frink explained. "We mostly have him make coffee."

"Really bad coffee," Zeeko added. "And I cut everyone's hair."

"He's pretty good at that," Lola said, and I had to admit her long curls were perfectly styled. Frink's green hair looked like a salad, but a well-tossed salad.

"I can make it look like Nlubglub has hair," Zeeko said, "but it takes forever."

"Um, okay." Making purple rubber look hairy would not have occurred to me. "Where's the rest of the crew?"

The four of them looked at one another, counting noses and/or noseless faces, then looked back at me.

I pictured the crew that served with my parents in the military. "Navigator? Engineer? Medical officer? Cook and bottle washer?"

"We don't have any of that," Zeeko said, still beaming at me. "When someone gets sick, I make them chicken soup. Except it's not really chicken; it's Ursan rugworm. It pretty much tastes the same."

Lola's aura turned blood red. "That was Ursan rugworm? Oh, now I'm really gonna be sick."

"So..." I summed up, "we have a ship with a hole in it, a crew of five, one of whom doesn't have a job description.... Is there anything else I should know?"

"We're pretty sure there's a Plutonian saboteur hiding somewhere on the ship," Lola said. "But it's okay; they don't eat much."

"Great," I said. They were all still looking at me expectantly. I tried to think of something captain-like to say. "So, um...carry on."

Lola's tone cut like a scalpel. "Haven't you forgotten something, Captain?"

I tried to match her delivery, but mine came out less scalpel and more butter knife. "What?"

"Don't you want to know our current mission?"

"Right. Of course."

Lola got up and walked to the computer. "We're supposed to be rescuing a Dr. Pilar Villarreal who's being held prisoner on Pluto right now."

"Pluto?" Nlubglub stretched halfway across the room to look over Lola's shoulder, which was disconcerting. "They couldn't send us someplace less miserable, like the center of a supernova inside a black hole?"

"Don't start," Lola said.

Nlubglub morphed back into the ball-with-feet shape. "It's not even a real planet."

I grabbed the first change of subject that came to mind. "When will the repairs be done so we can start the mission?"

"I'd say tomorrow at 08:00," Frink said.

Lola started back toward my chair. I squeezed in front of her and sat there first. She smirked, but I'd won this round. I was the captain, and we were all going to have to get used to that.

The chair made a screeching noise, and one arm detached itself and flew across the room, dials spinning.

"Tomorrow at 09:00," Frink corrected. The corners of his mouth were twitching, but he kept his voice steady. "That should give you time to fill out all the forms that have to be done before we leave."

"Right. I'll get started on that." I retreated to the corridor, then realized I had no idea where I was going. I stepped back in. "What's the name of this ship? It's not on any of the forms."

"There's a committee trying to decide on a name," Frink answered with an eye roll. "I think they have it narrowed down to the *Saint Willow Springs* or the *New Martian Harmony*."

Not again. This ship needed a name like the *Lemon*. Or the *It Seemed Like a Good Idea at the Time*. No, too long. "Until you hear otherwise, we're calling it the *Turkey*." I heaved my bag over my shoulder. "Someone show me where my quarters are?"

"This way." Nlubglub led me down another narrow passage, past a nest of exposed wiring that gave a disturbing hiss. "There isn't really a Plutonian saboteur. Lola's just messing with you."

"Good to know." I stopped as a realization hit me. "I forgot to ask for your pronouns." That's bad manners with several species, but a major faux pas with Jupiterans.

"I use 'they' and 'them,'" Nlubglub said pleasantly, stretching a little thinner to lead me around a tight corner.

"They? But there's only one of you."

Nlubglub chuckled. "There's definitely only one of me. If you prefer the Jupiteran version, it's 'plkzyft.' In more primitive languages like yours, 'they' is the closest approximation."

Primitive? I decided to let that pass. "Okay. My pronouns are 'she' and 'her.' And if you don't mind one more question, didn't Jupiterans call themselves Jovians up until a couple of years ago?"

"Yes, we change it every few decades. We live a long time, so we get bored. I change my own name every century or so."

The lights went out.

"You're sure there's no Plutonian saboteur?"

"Not totally sure, no."

The lights came back on as we arrived at my quarters. Nlubglub showed me how to unlock the door with my uniform insignia. I thanked them and went inside, tossing my bag on the bed. The room was in a color I would describe as "death gray," and just big enough for a bed, desk, and dresser. The computer had a viewscreen that was currently showing a motivational poster with a much fancier ship than mine and the words, *Aim high: even if you crash, it'll take you longer to hit the ground.*

The shelf over the bed held a few books—the archaic paper kind, not electronic ones—presumably left behind by a previous occupant. I scanned the titles: *Curling Not Hurling,* followed by *The Galactic Gourmet* and *The Space-Faring Moron's Guide to Common Science Fiction Plot Devices.* There was an electronic copy of the complete GUPPEAS regulations, since a paper copy probably would have killed whatever forests were left on Earth. I glanced at *Curling Not Hurling,* thinking it might help me with my hair, but it was about some kind of sport. I put it back.

The Space-Faring Moron's Guide to Common Science Fiction

Plot Devices looked well-thumbed. I pulled it down and scanned the introduction.

You're space-faring. You're a moron. You should have stayed home.

Not a promising beginning. I found the chapter on Jupiterans.

In science fiction, shapeshifters are able to perfectly mimic other species, changing not only their shape but also their weight and color. In spite of having no fixed form, they always come in exactly two genders. This is ridiculous, since the only actual shapeshifters are Jupiterans (previously known as Jovians, Jupiterers, or Jupiterese), and they have 46 different genders. Ten of these genders are referred to in English as "she," eight as "he," seven as "they," one as "y'all," one as "gzlfl," eighteen as "it," and one uses no personal pronouns. Jupiterans are able to change shape but not mass or color, so you really don't have to worry about one trying to steal your identity unless you're one bright color and your skin has a texture similar to vinyl. There is a legend of a mutated 47th gender that can convincingly imitate other species, even to the point of having a digestive tract, but that's just a spaceport legend like antimatter meta-mermaids.

"Good to know," I said out loud. I flipped a few more pages, checking out the chapter headings.

Starship captains: why they're always too young to be believable. Wise alien races. Hostile alien races. Alien races that need therapy. Inter-species romance. Security officers: why they should take out large insurance policies. Technological devices: always introduced right before they're needed. Paperwork. Faster-than-light travel: how to do it without reducing your innards to gravy. Pluto: not a real planet. Planets of scantily clad men.

Wait, there was a chapter on paperwork? I turned back to that section.

In science fiction, paperwork does not exist except in extremely dystopian cultures. If you've been assigned to complete any forms that can't be signed with your eyeballs, you're probably doomed. Also, no one can ever find a pen.

Not encouraging. I tried the chapter on planets of scantily clad men, which turned out to be brief:

The known universe of science fiction contains no planets of scantily clad men. There are planets of scantily clad women, all of whom are under age 30, apparently because they die young from pneumonia or hypothermia.

I started to shiver. No, it wasn't my imagination: the room had gotten cold. A few flakes of snow drifted down from the fire sprinkler. "Computer," I said, "turn the temperature up, please."

Nothing happened. I checked the environmental controls and couldn't find anything wrong. "Computer?"

The obvious next step was to ask one of the crew members. I cringed at the thought of looking like I didn't know what I was doing, especially when I didn't. Instead, I texted Martian with a picture of the control panel. Martian texted back: *It's set right. It's just ignoring you.*

He added, *Mom and Dad called. I told them you went for a drive and got stranded because the floatcar turned inside out. They believed it. But you might want to tell them what's going on.*

Oh, and don't read Pietro's blog. Seriously, don't.

My hand hovered over the beepity-beeper, a click away from looking up Pietro's blog. No. I wasn't going to let him have the satisfaction.

Instead I composed a message to my parents. *Hi, I've had this amazing opportunity. I'm sure you've heard of GUPPEAS, the peace organization. They not only wanted me to join; they made me a spaceship captain! It's a small ship, so new it doesn't even have a name yet. I was a little worried about leaving Martian by himself, but he'll have college to keep him busy, and the worst that'll happen is him inventing a robot to do his homework or something. I'll show you my captain's uniform as soon as I figure out how to send pictures on this state-of-the-art device. I'm really excited! Love, Janet.*

I couldn't bring myself to hit Send. Nothing in the message was technically a lie. ("Excited" could mean "panicking," right?) But it still felt wrong, so I saved a draft of the message to revise later.

I wrapped a blanket around me and reached for the forms. Now what had I done with that pen?

The next morning, the motivational poster on my viewscreen had changed to show a ship flying into a supernova: *Courage: it's what they call acts of dangerous stupidity if you survive them.* It was prettier than the old poster, but the rest of my quarters still qualified as death gray.

Somewhere between the travel authorization forms and the release of liability for meteor injuries the night before, I'd realized that no one was going to call and say this was all a mistake. I wasn't going to get out of being a spaceship captain. I deleted the message to my parents, wrote one that was closer to accurate, and hit Send.

The captain's uniform looked like it had been designed by a color-blind court jester: purple shirt, orange pants, yellow beret, glow-in-the-dark green boots, and a blue-and-gold braided sash that served no visible purpose. I put it on and headed for the bridge.

My four crew members were already there. All except Nlubglub were in their uniforms, similar to mine but with the colors reshuffled according to job function. Nlubglub settled for just the hat. Probably wanted to avoid the conspicuous red-shirted uniforms that security officers were supposed to wear, since according to *The Space-Faring Moron's Guide*, casualties had gone way up since those were instituted.

The tail of the ship looked, if not quite new, at least well patched. "How are the repairs going?" I asked, hoping I sounded vaguely captain-like.

Lola looked up from my chair. "They're done." She had accessorized her uniform with a spider-shaped gold hairpin that could probably double as a deadly weapon.

I touched the arm of the captain's chair. It stayed put, and so did Lola. I said, "Computer, what's our status?"

Silence.

"If everything's fixed, then why isn't the computer talking to me?"

"It's in a bad mood," Frink explained. "It's been giving us the silent treatment ever since it found out we don't have an engineer."

"It wasn't always in a great mood before that," Zeeko added. "They're going to try sending it to either a cryogenecist or a spiritual adviser next."

"Okay. When are we leaving for Pluto?" That didn't sound captain-like. Which one was the pilot? Frink, I was pretty sure. I looked over at him and tried again. "I mean, let's set a course for Pluto."

"What for?" Frink asked.

"For the mission. You remember—we talked about it yesterday. Rescuing that doctor."

They all looked at me like I'd turned into a Saturnian lizard-cow on a unicycle juggling pineapples with its horns. There were clearly questions required, but no one seemed to know what they were.

Zeeko said slowly, "We're going to do the mission?"

"Of course." I checked my reflection in the dark viewscreen to make sure I had not in fact turned into a Saturnian lizard-cow. "Why wouldn't we?"

"We've never done a mission before," Frink said. "Usually the captain starts on the paperwork, and then the mission gets canceled or changed, or made illegal, or they add new requirements like alphabetizing the numbers on the forms, and eventually we all go curling."

"Hurling?"

"No, curling," Nlubglub explained. "Hurling is a totally different sport. Curling is the one where you push a rock onto a patch of ice, and then two people with brooms try to sweep a path to the target." Nlubglub shapeshifted into a large broom, the hat still perched on top. "Want us to show you?"

"We're pretty good at it," Zeeko added. "Except when I forget and sweep in the wrong direction."

The skin around my temples started to tighten, the way it does when I'm about to make a huge mistake. What would a real captain do? "This time we'll change things up a little. Mission first, then hurling. Curling." The tightening became a full-fledged throb.

Lola chortled, and her aura sparkled with silver before returning to its usual pink. "Sure, that'll happen."

I tried to remember how to say Lola's full name. Finally I said, "First Officer, can I speak with you privately?"

Lola looked surprised, but she got up and followed me into the hallway. I shut the door behind us. "Do you have a problem with me?"

"Of course." She smirked at me while that sank in. "I have a problem with everyone, so don't go feeling like that makes you anything special."

"Well, we're stuck on this ship together." I crossed my arms, trying not to back down. "And it would be a whole lot easier if you quit undermining my orders. And when I'm on the bridge, that's my chair."

"Whatever. You won't be around for long. We've been through a dozen captains since I've been here." She elbowed past me, back onto the bridge.

"Right. Glad we got that straight." I followed her in. She walked to my chair, threw me another smirk, and kept walking to her station.

I took my seat. "What do we know about this doctor being held prisoner on Pluto?"

"There's a dossier." Nlubglub sent it to the small screen on my chair arm.

It only took me a minute to look over the information. "There's not a lot here. This Pilar Villarreal is some kind of public-health expert. It doesn't tell us what she was doing on Pluto or why the Plutonians are holding her."

Nlubglub's broad purple face curled into a sneer. "Who says the Plutonians need a reason to do something stupid?"

Pluto and Jupiter have been at war, on and off, for decades. Also, they riot at every badminton tournament. I said, "If we know the reason, then maybe there's a way we can get her out using negotiation and diplomacy."

"Or bribery," Frink offered.

"Or threats." That was Lola.

"Let's start with negotiation and diplomacy," I said. I'd gotten this far on unwarranted optimism; might as well stick with it for now. "So, um, let's go."

Everyone moved to their stations, then looked at me expectantly.

Finally Frink told me, "You're supposed to say, 'Launch.'"

"Right." I was hit with a wave of fear. What if the repairs weren't done right, and the ship fell apart? What if the engine stopped, and we were stuck drifting in space? What if my screwed-up relationship with technology ruined everything? What if a giant space squid decided we looked like a snack? What if we got to Pluto, and I had to figure how to make the mission a success?

What if I managed to act like a real captain, and the crew and Pietro and my teachers and everyone else had to deal with it?

"Launch."

The whole ship began to vibrate. I held my breath as the ground pushed away. There was a lurch, and then the ship was humming along, the town below us fading into the land mass and then the Earth itself growing smaller. No matter how many times I travel in space, there's something heart-stoppingly awesome about that moment of taking flight. If only the feeling could stay like this.

"Giant space squid at 300 parsecs," Lola said.

I nearly swallowed my tongue.

"She's kidding," Frink said. "Sit back and enjoy the ride."

Pluto was not most people's favorite place to travel. It was freezing cold, somewhere between absolute zero and the temperature of my ex-boyfriend's heart. Their idea of an exciting tourist destination was the Great Frozen River. Worldwide heating technology had improved parts of the planet from deadly to merely insufferable. The extra-light gravity required non-Plutonian visitors to use special weighted boots and ridiculous amounts of hairspray. Pluto's main industry was mining and processing fuelstone, which had replaced scarce fossil fuels for powering spaceships and other essentials. Plutonians had the biggest fuelstone supply in the galaxy, which was why other species tried to stay on good terms with them and not mention the fact that Pluto was too small to technically qualify as a real planet.

This not-planet was inhabited by scaly semi-reptilian humanoids with five antennae, and ruled by an Exalted Leader chosen through an arcane antenna-wrestling match among Pluto's most powerful warlords. Democracy had never been invented on this planet. Other things that were never invented there: jury trials, sarcasm, alphabetization, spam filters, sportsmanship, and chocolate. Tourism had improved slightly after they started importing chocolate.

All of which may explain why it took us two weeks to get to Pluto; I got the impression that nobody was in a hurry. The trip seemed even longer to me, because of the many strange quirks of the ship. Lights and environmental controls would go on and off for no reason, especially in my quarters in the middle of the night. The computer would emit colorful sparks or a burning smell. Sometimes it made a buzzing noise that sounded like a Morse code version of *get me a damned engineer, already.*

The laundry equipment devoured socks at an alarming rate. Frink blamed it on the Plutonian saboteur, but I said in that case the saboteur had a peg leg, because I never lost two from the same pair. I started rethinking the saboteur theory when other items started disappearing, like my favorite coffee mug and a titanium necklace that Pietro had given me. I'd probably misplaced the mug, since I didn't use it much after Martian built an alarm clock that injected coffee directly into my veins. But I couldn't imagine what had happened to the necklace, which I hadn't worn since Pietro broke up with me on prom night.

Pietro had always made fun of my supposed ability to destroy mechanical devices, but most of the time he treated it as an entertaining foible. When he asked me to prom, I didn't want to admit that I wasn't a very good dancer. Pietro was one of those terminally hip guys who knew the dances that everyone was doing before everyone started doing them.

So, I'd bought a ruffled lavender prom dress with indigo gloves and stockings, and a little technological help. Inside each article of clothing was a hidden computer chip programmed for all the latest moves. When the music started, the clothes would dance, and I'd follow along. What could go wrong?

Everything was fine for a few minutes. Pietro and I had some punch, chatted with friends, and talked about plans for post-graduation. Then the music started, just as I brushed against the sound system. And instead of sappy slow-dance music, it played Orion Thump-Crash-Metal.

This may or may not have been the reason I started flailing around like a sixteen-legged Neptunian globberbeast doing jumping jacks. And since I was holding on to Pietro, there was nothing he could do except follow along with me.

I clung to the hope that this was some trendy new dance that I hadn't heard of, or maybe a trend we were about to start. Then my body shifted into familiar flapping motions, and I realized what dance I was doing.

The Ditzy Space Owl.

Last year's most popular dance.

Which meant that the trend was over. Way over. So over that no one would even mention it anymore. And there we were, doing the Ditzy Space Owl in front of all of our friends.

Pietro never got over the humiliation. He demanded his ring back, and when the ring became magnetized and stuck to his belt, that just proved his point as far as he was concerned. He said never mind about returning the necklace.

And now, three months later, thinking about the missing necklace got me feeling maudlin about it. So, I did a stupid thing. I got on my computer and checked up on his blog, *Primarily Pietro.* I sat munching chocolate-covered popcorn, scrolling past the parts about famous people's fashion mistakes and driving while using telepathic communications devices (a pet peeve of his). Martian was right to warn me about it. This was Pietro's idea of clever, soulful writing:

DISASTER ON TWO SHORT LEGS

You know what it's like the first day after getting over the flu, when you rediscover how good it feels to breathe freely and get up without wanting to keel over?

That's pretty much how it feels after breaking up with Jam-it Delane.

Earthlings are a disappointing bunch in general, but this specimen is a short, ten-pounds-overweight creature with a shapeless mass of hair that is not quite brown and not quite black. Despite her small size, she has a large voice and makes ample use of it.

The woman is a walking Red Alert. She draws disaster to her like a Betelgeusian boxfly to a flame, only without the box-fly's grace. She can make any technological device implode just by being in the general vicinity. Sooner or later some corporation will hire her to stand in their rival's lobby and cause all the computers to expel their core processors and catapult them around the room.

"That thing with the computer only happened once!" I yelled at nobody. "And it was only because I'd been exposed to that weird anti-radiation at work." And who *wasn't* ten pounds overweight? Big voice, I'd show him a big voice. "Idiot!" I couldn't believe this was the same guy I'd adored when he was a high school volleyball star. I reached for another handful of popcorn, then put it back.

There was a horrendous picture of me doing the Ditzy Space Owl, with Pietro's image carefully edited out.

In my next entry, I'll tell you all about Thanksgiving dinner with her gadget-obsessed brother.

UPDATE: I have just learned that Jam-il has joined GUPPEAS, at the rank of Captain, no less. One can only assume that in the next few days the entire organization will be destroyed by some combination of radioactive leprosy and—

"Captain!" Nlubglub's voice chirped on my beepity-beeper. "We've arrived at Pluto, the most miserable place in this universe or any other."

"Thank goodness," I said.

3

Disappearing Socks

Exalted Leader's palace on Pluto was the size of my whole neighborhood back home. According to the briefing we got from Nlubglub, it contained an assortment of offices, living quarters, guards, servants, government officials, a ballroom, and an extensive dungeon underneath. The first thing I noticed, as the half-dozen guards escorted us in, was that it was as freezing cold inside as it was outside. The guards, who looked a bit like toad-humanoid hybrids, were wearing only loincloths. I shivered just looking at them. Each carried a giant spear that looked more ceremonial than practical, and a holstered gun.

I'd brought the entire crew except for Nlubglub, figuring that their hostility toward Pluto could be a hindrance to diplomacy. We stumbled along between the guards, each crew member wearing weighted boots designed to keep us on the ground in the slight Plutonian gravity. The boots were already driving me crazy, both because they forced an awkward lurching walk and because they were a distracting fluorescent green.

Inside, the place smelled like mildew. A gooey brown mold grew on the walls, dripping from the banners that hung in every room with the official motto, "Pluto: Realest of the Real Planets."

The guards stopped outside the audience chamber, raised their antennae at attention, and burst into song.

Exalted Leader,
He's the ruler supreme!
His glory is massive,
His honor extreme!

Exalted Leader,
Ruler of Pluto,
Realest of planets,
The one we all want to go to!

"That doesn't even rhyme," Frink muttered. Lola silenced him with a look.

They led us into the audience chamber, where Exalted Leader stood on a platform two steps higher than the rest of the room. He was a pudgy, floppy-faced Plutonian in a mossy shade of dark green. His drab military uniform sported a variety of medals in gold and aluminum.

"Greetings, Your Exaltedness." It felt like I had to unstick each word from my throat. "My name is Janet Delane."

"Captain," Lola whispered sharply.

"Captain Janet Delane," I corrected myself. "We've come from GUPPEAS. My crew and I wish to request the release of a citizen of Earth. Dr. Pilar Villarreal."

Exalted Leader stared down at me, his dark eyes bulging, jowls quivering. I had no idea if he was going to say yes or order us all into the dungeon. In his frozen palace on the coldest planet in the galaxy, I was sweating so hard, it was turning to steam.

"Do you know who you're dealing with here?"

"Um...yes?" Never mind that I didn't know his actual name, which wasn't in the file.

"I am the ruler of the most important planet in the universe!" He started pointing at his various medals. "I got this for valor in the last war against Jupiter. And this one for naming a new holiday: Exalted Leader Day. And this one for sneezing on an enemy soldier and giving him an incapacitating cold. And this one...wait, what was this one for?"

"Winning a pasta-cooking contest, m'lord," said one of his advisers. The advisers were in white uniforms and even floppier-faced than he was.

"Right. Anyway, point is, I'm not someone you can trifle with."

"Of course," Lola said. "And it's precisely because you're so important that releasing a lowly Earthling prisoner would win the admiration of people far and wide."

Wait, Lola could be diplomatic? Why had I not known this?

I added, "In fact, that's exactly the sort of heroic deed that would deserve a new medal."

It was hard to tell with a fish-like face, but I think Exalted Leader's eyes lit up. He gestured for the advisers to come closer, and huddled in a whispered discussion with them.

"Do you think those medals are valuable?" Frink whispered while the Plutonians were distracted.

Lola's aura turned crimson. "Don't even think about it."

Before I could ask what that was about, Exalted Leader turned his attention back to us. "We know of this Dr. Villarreal. She has committed a serious violation, and we are not prepared to release her."

I sniffed, trying not to let my nose run in the cold. "Can we see her? That way we can report back on how she's being treated."

"Of course we're not suggesting any sort of mistreatment," Lola added quickly. "But you know how it is with bureaucrats. We need to be able to report back that we saw her condition for ourselves."

After another lengthy consultation, Exalted Leader—I'll bet his real name was Nerdson Junior or something—sent a pair of guards to bring the prisoner.

I asked, "What exactly was the nature of her offense?"

"She broke the Ban!" he thundered. You could hear the capital letter in "the Ban." It was the sort of tone used for deep, centuries-old taboos.

The guards returned with a bedraggled-looking older woman in crooked spectacles. She slipped on a moldy patch on the floor and lost her balance. Her glasses started to float away, and she grabbed for them, inadvertently launching herself into the air. I tried to catch her, which sent us both flying in slow motion into the wall, where we slid down in an undignified heap.

I pulled myself to my feet and helped her up, trying not to look at the snickering Plutonians. "We're from GUPPEAS. Are you all right?"

She managed a wan smile. Seen up close, she was younger than she'd first appeared—in her forties, maybe. "I've had better weeks."

"Did they hurt you?"

"No, it's just the food. I've never been this long without chocolate."

"Maybe we can get her a care package while we're negotiating?" I suggested to her captors.

The guards stared at me open-mouthed. Exalted Leader waddled closer until his gray-green face was two inches from mine. "Chocolate is Banned!"

A collective gasp ran through my crew. "That's impossible," Frink stammered. "Nobody bans chocolate!"

"Even the Jupiterans wouldn't do that," Lola added, "and they don't even eat."

"Have you even tried chocolate?" Zeeko asked Exalted Leader. "It's really good."

"It is delectable!" Exalted Leader roared back. "And I can't eat it! It gives me hives! Horrible, painful, itchy hives on my whole body!"

"You're allergic," Dr. Villarreal said. "But that doesn't mean all Plutonians are."

"I don't care! If I can't have it, no one can!" He stomped his squishy feet. "If I could ban it on other planets, I'd do that too! And this human had contact with the smuggler who's been sneaking in contraband. We caught her eating an entire chocolate cupcake."

"I couldn't help it," Dr. Villarreal said weakly.

I elbowed her, almost causing her to float away again. "I'm sure she will promise never to do it again."

Exalted Leader was unimpressed. "She won't tell us how to find the smuggler."

"There's nothing to tell," Dr. Villarreal said. "The smuggler found me. I don't know how."

"And you ate the evidence. How convenient."

"I ate it because it was chocolate." A dreamy look crossed her face. "And delicious."

One of the guards began coughing uncontrollably and keeled over, his body twitching like a fish trying to escape the hook.

Dr. Villarreal knelt down next to him. "Chocolate withdrawal," she said. "Needs a carob patch. If you've still got my medical bag, it should be in there." Two of the other guards picked up the sick one and carried him off to the infirmary.

"See, she just helped one of your people," I said. "Obviously she means you no harm. And in the spirit of interplanetary cooperation, not to mention interplanetary commerce, I'm sure we can work out an agreement that satisfies everyone. We'll even buy some extra fuelstone to get out of here at top speed."

Exalted Leader thought this over. "Tell you what. I will pardon the doctor if you and your crew will catch the smuggler who brought in the chocolate."

I had not the vaguest idea how we were supposed to do that. Or even if we should.

"Okay," I said.

Back on the ship, I gathered the crew on the bridge. "Anyone have ideas for how to catch a smuggler?"

"The Plutonians already have patrol ships in orbit." Nlubglub pulled up an image of the route onscreen. "Somehow the smuggler is getting past them."

"Probably just gives them chocolate," Zeeko said.

Lola narrowed her eyes at him. "It worries me when you start making sense."

Nlubglub traced an area on the map. "This seems like a likely spot. Minimal patrols, and close to large population centers where customers will be easy to find."

"Which means the smuggler will more likely be over here." Frink pointed to an area above the Great Frozen River. "Access is almost as good, and they'll be expecting an ambush in the other spot."

"I'd go with Frink on this one," Lola said.

Nlubglub considered. "You may be right."

I looked over at Zeeko. "Any thoughts?"

"Why don't we just tell them we want to buy some chocolate, and let them come to us?"

"Because we can't tell them if we can't find them."

"Oh. Right."

There followed two weeks of alternating frustration and boredom while we patrolled in a low orbit. Each time we thought we'd spotted an unauthorized ship, it turned out to be space debris, or a slightly off-course fuelstone freighter, or a giant space squid (which, fortunately, wasn't fast enough to catch us). Lola kept muttering about needing to "crack some heads and then go meditate."

On day fifteen, we nearly got blown out of the sky by a Plutonian patrol ship that mistook us for the smuggler. I was in desperate need of a hot fudge sundae to calm my nerves, but the Plutonians had removed every trace of chocolate on the ship before we'd left the planet. To top it off, my coffee-injecting alarm clock had disappeared. I was about ready to throw somebody against a wall.

Maybe there really was a Plutonian saboteur on board. Where would they hide my alarm clock? (And why would they need one— don't saboteurs get to set their own schedules?) I searched the laundry room and the shuttle bay, eventually winding up in the engine room.

Normally, the twin pillars of the engine throbbed in unison, one with white fuelstone swirling in light matter, the other with black fuelstone in dark matter. Today, I could hear a strange syncopated rhythm. A moment later, the hatch began sputtering, giving off rainbow-colored sparks. I moved in for a closer look. As soon as I touched the knob, there was a nasty sound from inside the walls, something between a *kerpow* and a *whump*.

The ship stopped dead in space.

I put out a call for crew assistance in the engine room, and Frink, Lola, and Nlubglub came racing in. "Wait," I asked, "Zeeko's flying the ship?"

"It's not exactly flying at the moment, so it doesn't matter," Frink said. "Remind me again why we don't have an engineer?" He climbed up the hatch with Nlubglub in tow. The noises that followed sounded like somebody torturing a floatcar alarm.

"Maybe you shouldn't stand so close," Lola told me. "I think that guy Pietro might have a point about you and machinery."

I started to protest, but just then the engines growled back to life, and we fell into each other as the ship started moving again.

Frink emerged barefoot and grimy, his leafy green hair covered in a layer of soot. "I think we got hit by a gravity well. We'll have to move to a higher orbit."

"What for? The smuggler's not here." Nlubglub bounced down out of the hatch, then reached up to secure the cover. "I knew this was the wrong place. You should have listened to me; I'm the security chief."

"But you agreed with me about this spot," Frink said. "You all did."

"We thought you knew what you were talking about," Lola snapped. "Since you know how criminals think."

Frink turned on her, orange eyes flashing. "Are you calling me a criminal?"

Lola's aura rippled. "Of course."

Frink got right up in her face. "And you're not one?"

I stepped forward. "Can we all take it down a notch?"

"Go back to high school." Lola's aura brightened to a furious red.

"And take your stupid mission with you," Frink added.

"I'm the captain, and if you're insubordinate, I'll—I'll..." What was I even authorized to do?

"I'll throw all of you in the brig," Nlubglub said.

It happened fast, and I'm not completely sure who threw the first punch, but I wound up on the floor while Frink and Lola were pounding on each other. Nlubglub sprouted a few extra arms to hold them both down. Somehow in the fracas, Lola's sash and Frink's boots both wound up being pulled off and stuck halfway into Nlubglub's head.

"They'll be fine in a minute," Nlubglub told me, keeping them both pinned. "Everyone's on edge because we've never done a mission before, and this one isn't going too well."

"I'd be fine if I had some chocolate," Lola growled. "You don't understand because Jupiterans don't eat."

"And I hate being called a criminal," Frink said.

"Usually you don't mind." Nlubglub released them and morphed back into their usual giant-tennis-ball-with-legs shape.

"Oh. Right." Frink sat up and reached for his boots.

My mouth fell open. He was wearing my titanium necklace, the one from Pietro, as an ankle bracelet.

"Frink," I said, "what are you doing with my necklace?"

"I don't know what you're talking about." He hastily pulled up his mismatched socks.

"That chain you have around your ankle, with the little heart pendant. Everyone saw it. That's my necklace, and it disappeared out of my quarters three weeks ago."

"I found it."

"In my quarters? This isn't some creepy stalker thing, is it?"

"He's a kleptomaniac." Lola retrieved her sash and began tidying her hair. "You know GUPPEAS is made up of all criminals."

"Come again?"

Lola spoke slowly, possibly to imply that I was an idiot for not knowing this—or maybe she was just slowing down from chocolate deprivation. "You joined GUPPEAS because of your little traffic accident or whatever it was, and you didn't want to go to jail. Nlubglub was in the billiard riot that started the last war with Pluto."

"They totally cheated," Nlubglub said. "Even in zero-g, you have to keep one foot on the floor."

"Nlubglub didn't want to go to jail either, so hello, Peacemongering Spacefleet. And Frink's a compulsive pickpocket and occasional burglar."

"Both perfectly respectable occupations on my home planet," Frink said. "Most people in my family run pyramid schemes or email frauds. How was I supposed to know that on other planets you're not allowed to steal houses?"

I held out my hand until Frink took off the necklace and laid it in my palm. Not wanting to wear it—it had come from Pietro, after all—I stuffed it in my pocket. "Everyone's here because they're a felon?"

"More like misdemeanorans," Frink said.

"Except maybe Zeeko," Nlubglub added. "We never did figure out how he got here."

I turned to Lola. "What did you do?"

She moved a little closer. "I beat up my boss for asking too many nosy questions."

I tried not to think about the fact that, technically, I was now her boss. "And you were sentenced to join a peace organization?"

"That and lots of meditation. I think using a meditation crystal is helping. If I ever run into my old boss again, I'll probably only leave him hospitalized for half as long."

I swallowed. "Good to know."

Later that evening, I marched Frink to his quarters, where he returned my mug, some silverware, and a reading light. He denied having taken my alarm clock. "Look around." He spread his arms out wide. "Do you see it?"

I didn't. I saw about thirty wristwatches, an illegal interplanetary police scanner, a turntable for vinyl records, a large orange gem, books on various crimes including a how-to for hotwiring spaceships, a tiny building possibly stolen from Lilliputians, a change jar full of currency from various planets (including one that used bird feet for money), and a bookcase full of curling stones with polished handles, several of which were inscribed with *Goo-Goo Baby Food.*

"The Goo-Goo Baby Food Company owns a sports arena?"

"No," he said, "a penitentiary. All the good naming rights were already taken."

"Ah." I looked again at the orange gem. "That's not Lola's meditation crystal, is it?"

"Oh no. I'm never coming between her and that again." He shuddered. "No, this is just the legendary Lost Jewel of Togmagog. Took it off an old boyfriend. Girlfriend? I forget now. I usually date guys, but women and nonbinaries have better stuff to steal. My last boyfriend was an artist, so I took a bunch of his paint and some brushes and repainted my quarters. He was kind of upset about it, though."

I had to admit the walls were a nice pattern in varying shades of blue, instead of the ghastly gray of my quarters. "Maybe you'd have better luck with romantic partners if you didn't steal from them."

"Really?" He looked like that idea had never occurred to him. "I'm not sure I should be taking relationship advice from someone whose ex-boyfriend has a blog calling her Jam-it the Technology-Slayer."

I stiffened. "Does the whole crew read that blog?"

"I'm not sure Zeeko reads."

I turned and saw a pile of socks in the corner. "Whose are those?"

"Mine." He held up a handful, and none of them looked like the ones I was missing. "Those are the ones whose mates disappeared in the laundry. You're not the only one who loses them."

"Likely story," I said. "The mismatched socks probably go better with the uniform colors anyway. But that coffee-injecting clock is on loan from my brother, and I want it back."

"I'm telling you, I don't have any—"

"How did you get this?" I picked up a medal. It was kind of generic, but it looked suspiciously like the ones Exalted Leader had been wearing.

"It's been two weeks, and he hasn't noticed. I figured I'd sell it back to him as a new one."

"That's ridiculous."

"More ridiculous than telling him one of your crew swiped it?"

I added the medal to my pile of reclaimed items. "I'll think of something. And what's this?" I picked up a thumb-sized device with a tiny dial. I'd seen pictures of similar items in the news. "This is some kind of electronic lockpick, isn't it? These are totally illegal."

"Um, I know it sort of looks like one, but it's actually a cyber mosquito repellant."

"Cyber mosquitoes?"

"You don't see any in here, do you?" His voiced oozed sincerity. "In fact, for a small fee, I can sell you one so that cyber mosquitoes don't show up in your quarters either."

"Captain," came Lola's voice over the beepity-beeper, "we've got an unknown ship onscreen."

I pocketed the lockpick and ran to the bridge.

4

Chicken That Tasted Like Dried Regelworm

I strode onto the bridge and stood over Lola until she vacated my chair. I sat. "Lola, hail the ship."

"I'm not the communications officer." The edge in her voice was sharp enough to replace commercial razors.

I tried to sound authoritative, but it came out in a squeak. "We don't have a communications officer."

She yawned. "Zeeko can do it. It's not like we'd be keeping him from anything else."

"Um, sure." Zeeko wandered over to the communications panel. "What button do I push?"

I got up and pushed the button myself. "This is Captain Janet Delane of…" I glanced at the logo on the computer to get it right, "the Galactic Universal Peacemongering Paradigm Emergent Action Spacefleet."

"How nice for you," said a cheerful female voice from the other ship. Much too lively for someone orbiting a planet with no chocolate. Was it my imagination, or was the ship the same color as a dark chocolate bar?

"Please identify yourself."

"I'm a little busy," she said with a sly giggle. "I'm in the middle of dessert, and I like to enjoy my chocolate. Maybe later."

Before I could respond, Lola said, "We're going to board your ship right now!"

More laughter. "Why, are you hungry?"

"No," I said, "you're under arrest!"

We were already in the shuttlecraft before I realized the person we'd left behind to run the ship was Nlubglub—the only one who didn't eat. Too late now. We landed in the alien ship's shuttle bay. Frink cracked the lock-code on the cargo hold almost instantly. I left him and Zeeko there to look for evidence, and took Lola with me to the bridge.

On the bridge, we found a young woman lounging in the command chair with a bowl in her hand. The chocolate smell was so luscious, I had to stop several feet away from her.

"Who the hell are you?" I demanded.

"I the hell am Captain Nina Mikeljohn of the independent ship *Mariposa.*" She popped a bite into her mouth, chewed slowly, and swallowed. She held the bowl toward us. "Truffle? Chocolate cherry? Chocolate-covered asparagus heart?"

"Captain Mikeljohn—"

"Oh, please. It's Nina. You're Janet, right?"

Lola punched the name and registration into her beepity-beeper. "There's no record of you or your ship."

"Oh, well. I guess if I don't exist, you can't arrest me." She stood up. She was far too skinny for a chocolate smuggler. At first glance she looked like a teenager, with a girlish face surrounded by dirty-blonde waves. But something in her eyes suggested she'd lived a very long, very crafty life. Centuries, maybe. Her eyes were aqua and too bright, like the headlights of a ship emerging from a black hole.

"Where's the rest of your crew?" I asked.

"I'm it." Nina, or whatever her real name was, gave the bowl of chocolates a little shake. Lola's hand was moving, as if of its own accord, toward the forbidden sweets.

I smacked Lola's arm down. "You can't bring chocolate to Pluto. And that includes ships orbiting Pluto. It's a stupid law, and the whole population is pretty depressed about it, but it's still the law."

"Rough break for you," Nina Mikeljohn observed. "You join a spacefleet that's supposed to be about peace, and you wind up in charge of depriving a whole planet of the most divine food ever created, all because its Exalted Leader is a narcissistic, control-crazed regelworm who would ban happiness if he could figure out a way to do it." She dangled a piece of fudge, cocking an eyebrow at Lola. "And there's ten pounds of chocolate-covered espresso beans in the hold."

Lola's eyes seemed to be trying to pull the chocolate closer while her aura struggled back and forth between light and dark. I made every effort to stay focused, but that was hard when the whole bridge smelled like chocolate. And not the cheap candy-bar type, but the gourmet dark chocolate that probably originated in some secret underground confectionary on Neptune. The smell was beckoning me like an impassioned lover, taunting, alluring, begging me to reach for it.

Nina eyebrowed a question at me.

"We don't make the rules," I said weakly. "We just have to enforce them. We're professionals."

Lola seized the bowl and stuffed all the chocolate down her throat before I could move.

Zeeko and Frink came bouncing into the room. "Captain! Guess what!"

"What?" Nina and I said simultaneously.

Zeeko was speaking at light speed. "No-chocolate-hold-I-mean-in-the-hold-no-evidence-whatsoever-nothing-to-confiscate-Frink-said-to-tell-you-there-was."

I palmed my forehead. "You ate the chocolate espresso beans, didn't you?"

"Not all of them. Frink ate some."

Nina wiped her mouth. "Guess there's no contraband, then." She stood up and stretched. "Next time, Janet, you might want to move faster so you get some too. Goodbye for now."

"Wait," I said. "They're holding one of our people prisoner for eating chocolate. They won't let her go unless we arrest you." I felt idiotic as soon as the words were out; obviously, Nina wasn't going to turn herself in. I braced for another sarcastic remark.

Instead, she gave me a thoughtful look. "Have you tried appealing to his ego? People who call themselves Exalted Leader usually go for that sort of thing. And I happen to know his real name is Fibbreous Nekwizzle."

Frink was searching the bridge for any more hiding places for chocolate, while Zeeko continued racing around the room.

"Maybe decaf espresso beans next time?" I said wanly. "Look, help us out here. There's an innocent person sitting in the Exalted Leader's dungeon because you smuggled this contraband in."

"Innocent?" Nina licked a last spot of fudge off her finger. "She had chocolate, same as me."

"Um, sure, but—"

"Try calling the ambassador that GUPPEAS sends for these situations. I hear he's pretty good, and it's much cheaper than mounting a full-blown rescue." She started walking us back to the shuttle. "If you do have to mount a full-blown rescue, give me a call first. I might be able to help."

"And you'd do what? Drop chocolate on them?"

She snickered. "I'd never waste good chocolate that way. But I have a few skills."

"You know we could just arrest you, right?"

"Unfortunately, your crew ate all the evidence," she said. We'd reached the shuttle bay by now. "And the kind of probing that would find it would be very uncomfortable, not to mention that it would make your crew look very guilty."

After that, there was nothing to do but return to the *Turkey* and give a highly edited report to Vertin Bogler, the Venusian bureaucrat who'd signed me up for GUPPEAS. He said he'd personally escort the ambassador here. Apparently, that had been the original plan instead of sending us, but somebody's assistant's assistant had misplaced the right forms.

"I hate ambassadors," Lola griped after the call ended. "They're always about two hundred years old and they never stop talking. I think they negotiate treaties by promising to shut up and go away."

That was pretty much my impression of ambassadors, too. I'd met a couple of them on the ship where my parents served. Which reminded me: I should send my parents another message to update them. They'd responded to my last one: *You'll be a great captain. Don't worry if you make a few mistakes—our captain nearly tied the universe into an endless time-travel loop last week.*

Which didn't make me feel any more confident about dealing with Exalted Leader.

A few days later, the Plutonians threw a reception to welcome the ambassador, if "welcome" is the right word when the festivities started with an address from Exalted Leader about the wonderfulness of Exalted Leader. My crew all managed to disappear by the end of the speech. I wound up lurking by the punch bowl, looking around for the unlucky new arrival, but I didn't see any centenarians. Instead I ran into Vertin Bogler, his aura still glowing that smarmy lime green. Maybe it was always that color. "Hello, Captain," he said. "How are you liking your assignment?"

"Fine," I said, which is probably the sort of lie that gets people punished for several afterlives. "I did have a couple of questions. Like about Zeeko. What exactly is his job function supposed to be?"

"Zeeko? There's nobody by that name assigned to your ship."

"But he was there when I—"

"Oh, here comes the ambassador. Good evening, Ambassador Dangere."

"Anything good at the buffet?" asked a deep, pleasant voice behind me.

I turned and saw the handsomest man in this galaxy or any other. He was maybe twenty-two years old, with curly dark hair and a tan face that seemed to mix the best of all of Earth's continents at once. His eyes were arresting, as blue as the sky would have been if the Plutonian sky wasn't green. While everyone else was wearing a garish GUPPEAS uniform or a pond-scum-colored Plutonian one, he looked elegant in a tuxedo.

"Sorry, didn't mean to sneak up behind you," he said. "I'm Ambassador Dangere. Please call me Beau."

I stood breathless, wanting to say something witty about devouring his full gorgeous lips, except of course you can't say that sort of thing to strangers at an alien buffet.

He smiled, oblivious to the effect he had. "Should I repeat the question?"

I found my voice. "Buffets are pretty much all the same everywhere. Dried regelworm that tastes like chicken, some indistinguishable fruits, and chicken that tastes like dried regelworm." Great, I was trying to be witty, and this was what I came in with? I wanted to kick myself, but only after tying myself to a chair and perching on the edge of the roof on a very high building.

"And if we'd left you on the job a day longer, there'd have been chocolate as well." That wasn't him talking, though, unless he'd suddenly developed a woman's voice. Nope: the woman was coming up beside me. She was unusually tall, made even taller by a knot of auburn hair perched atop her head. She wore a dark-blue uniform that was perfectly tailored for her.

Beau Dangere gave me a conspiratorial look. "In that case, how about staying on?"

"Not funny," the woman said. "I can't believe they can't even catch one smuggler. Good thing my crew's replacing these losers."

"Excuse me," I said. "You are…?"

"Captain Richena Rossi, of course."

I tried not to stare at her hair, and the way it all stayed in place while everyone else's was floating in every direction in the low gravity. "And you said something about replacing…?"

"Er, yes," said Bogler. I had forgotten he was there. "I was getting around to that. Captain Rossi's ship will be taking over the search for the smuggler." He gave her a quizzical look that lightened his aura ever so slightly. "That doesn't seem to be a standard uniform, Captain Rossi."

"It's my own design," she said airily. "I haven't gotten any memos telling me to change it. Now, where's Exalted Leader?" She took Bogler's arm and led him across the room, working the crowd like a politician.

Beau stayed behind. "So as long as no one's listening," he said, "what kind of chocolate was it?"

My heart melted like chocolate chips in a cookie fresh from the oven. "You name it, she had it. Dark chocolate, milk chocolate, truffles, fudge."

"But none of that white chocolate crap, right?"

"Come on. That's not even real chocolate." I was feeling bolder now that we'd found something to agree on. "Aren't you a little young for an ambassador?"

"Because they're always at least four hundred years old? I think the one from Saturn is seven hundred, and that's Saturnian years." Beau took a bite of something from the buffet and frowned as if he were trying to figure out whether it was chicken or dried regelworm. "I was interning at GUPPEAS Command Central when this position opened up, and no one else wanted it because there was no chocolate. Richena says she doesn't see what the big deal is—she doesn't like chocolate all that much."

"How weird," I said. "And she looks just like an Earthling."

He chuckled. "Trust me, I've been through enough breakups and makeups with her—she's definitely an Earthling."

I tried not to be obvious about looking at his hand. No wedding ring.

"Hey!" Zeeko came running toward me. "We got an urgent message about Dr. Villarreal. I'll be right back!" He whooshed past before I could ask any questions.

"Your date?" Beau asked.

"What? Oh no. He's one of my crew—I think he is, anyway."

"Well then, he won't mind if we dance." Beau's blue eyes glittered like gems. (Sapphires, I guess. The only other blue gemstones I could think of were turquoises—turquoii?—and they don't really glitter.) "Try turning your gravity boots off."

I did, and my feet barely touched the ground as I followed him to the dance floor, where Richena was chatting up the members of the Plutonian council.

Dancing with Beau on a planet with one-twelfth of Earth's gravity was the next best thing to waltzing on air. And since my uniform wasn't programmed for dance moves, I let him lead.

Over by the window, a human-shaped figure was standing in the shadows. It looked familiar. Nina Mikeljohn? No, that couldn't be right—what would she be doing here?

We waltzed past Richena, close enough that I could hear a lawyerish-looking Plutonian ask her, "So, Captain Rossi, what exactly is it that you have in that sealed-off storage bay in your ship?"

"Oh, nothing." That breezy tone seemed to be her signature. "We're just doing some repairs on a damaged shuttle in there."

"Really? Because I heard a rumor that it was filled with—"

Beau spun me around, away from Richena, and I tripped over my boots but managed not to cause any major injuries.

"What was that about?" I asked.

"What was what about?"

"Something about a sealed-off storage bay on Captain Rossi's ship. She's not hiding chocolate up there, is she?"

"That'll be the day." He laughed softly, his breath warm in my ear. "So, what crime did you commit to get into GUPPEAS? Had to be a pretty good one to make captain."

Crime had never sounded so sexy before. "Wanton and mildly atrocious…something."

"Wanton, eh?" He gave me another spin. I wasn't sure if my light-headed feeling was because of the minimal gravity, or because Beau's arms were the first warmth I'd felt since arriving on Pluto.

I cleared my throat. "You said you and Richena had breakups and makeups—which one are you on right now?"

Zeeko reappeared beside me, almost knocking me over. "Captain, you're not gonna believe it!"

"What?"

"Dr. Villarreal thinks she may have the cure for Exalted Leader's allergy. He said to bring the ambassador and the captain to the laboratory right away."

Richena elbowed her way between Beau and me, taking his arm. "We'd better go, then."

"Right." I tried to turn the gravity boots back on, but the switch was frozen in place. I gave up and floated after them.

We took the elevator down to the bottom level. The complex got colder the lower we went. I could hear snatches of conversation from around the corner.

"I was just casing—I mean exploring—the complex." The man's voice was familiar.

The woman laughed. "Same here."

We turned and passed Frink, who was cozying up to Nina Mikeljohn. He was touching her arm with one hand while his other hand slid into her pocket. Wait, shouldn't I turn her in for smuggling? But there was no evidence that she had any chocolate; my crew had made sure of that. And if Exalted Leader's allergy was cured, chocolate smuggling wouldn't matter anymore.

The laboratory was up ahead. I kept walking alongside Beau and Richena, pretending I hadn't noticed Frink and Nina in the hallway. Zeeko said nothing, smiling obliviously.

We filed into the lab, where Exalted Leader sat at a high table. A half-dozen guards lined the walls, each holding a weapon that looked like a stuffed swordfish. A few other Plutonians stood off to the side, including some of his advisers and a servant with a covered dish. Dr. Villarreal looked in her element, dressed in a white coat with her glasses threatening to fall off the end of her nose.

"It's just about ready." She began filling a syringe.

"This had better work," Exalted Leader whined. "You have no idea how hard it's been for me, doing without chocolate."

"Of course we do." Zeeko looked puzzled. "You haven't let any of us have chocolate either."

I elbowed Zeeko. "In fact, you've made us so appreciative of your hardship that GUPPEAS wishes to award you this medal for your courage and forbearance in a state of chocolatelessness." I reached into my pocket and pulled out the medal that I'd retrieved from Frink's quarters.

Exalted Leader's eyes lit up as he examined it. "Excellent workmanship." His antenna twitched. "It looks familiar."

"Yes." I thought fast. "We used a style that we knew you liked, so that it would harmonize with your other medals."

"Perfect." He gestured to one of the guards, who came over and pinned it on him.

"Good thinking," Beau whispered, grinning at me. Suddenly, the room didn't seem cold at all.

Dr. Villarreal readied the syringe. "This won't hurt a bit." She jabbed the needle into the base of his antenna.

Exalted Leader's scream knocked icicles off the ceiling.

Two of the guards grabbed Dr. Villarreal and pulled her away. "Sorry," she said. "I thought everyone knew that's how doctors say it's going to hurt." After a moment, the guards let her go.

Exalted Leader rubbed his antenna with one hand, and beckoned to the servant with the other. The servant brought the dish to the table and uncovered its contents: chocolate mousse and a cup of coffee. Exalted Leader scooped up a generous spoonful and, after the briefest hesitation, put it in his mouth and swallowed.

I was halfway across the room, and the smell of chocolate was tormenting me.

"No hives!" He looked at his arm with wonder. "I feel fine. I'm cured." He stood up and spread his arms. "Chocolate is Unbanned!"

Cheers broke out all over the room and down the hall. Everyone grabbed and kissed the nearest person. Or at least, I did. And Beau was the nearest person.

The kiss stopped clocks. It stopped time. It stopped my heart and started it again.

A perfectly manicured hand yanked me away from Beau and shoved me toward the door. And because we were in Plutonian gravity, the momentum carried me out into the hallway. "Oops," Richena said with a smirk.

I landed in front of a surprised Frink and Nina. Nina was in the middle of handing back Frink's monogrammed wallet.

"Wait," he said, "when did you take this?" He looked impressed.

From inside the lab, I heard a Plutonian voice ask, "Ambassador Dangere, is everything all right?"

"Fine," Beau said.

"Excuse us a minute." That was Richena. A moment later she and Beau emerged from the room. She had his arm in a death grip and kept her voice down. Frink, Nina, and I pretended we couldn't hear.

"Beau, we talked about this," Richena hissed.

"I know." He looked away, red-faced. "I just got caught up in the moment."

I forgot I wasn't supposed to be listening. "It wasn't his fault. It was me that kissed him."

Richena looked at me like an Orion dragon about to devour its prey. "This is none of your business."

A shriek erupted from the lab, ten times worse than Exalted Leader's scream earlier. We all ran back in.

Exalted Leader had orange blotches all over his greenish-gray skin. He was shaking violently, sitting with his hands wrapped around his coffee cup, sloshing coffee all over the place.

Dr. Villarreal peered in his mouth and checked the pulse in his antenna. "Looks like the cure gave you a secondary allergy to caffeine."

He looked up at her, antennae shaking. "So I can't have coffee?"

"Coffee, tea, some sodas, and, um…chocolate has caffeine as well."

"Oh no," Beau and I said simultaneously. Our eyes locked, dreading what was coming next.

Exalted Leader wobbled to his feet. "Everything with caffeine is Banned!"

"I'm on it," Nina whispered to me. "I'll run over to Buck's Star and be right back." She raced out the door.

"Hurry!" I called after her.

5

Cup Holders Inside the Cup Holders

A few days later, fighting my caffeine cravings, I wandered past the coffee shop down the street from Exalted Leader's palace. The shop was locked up with a chain on the door, but the windows were smashed, and everything inside had been stolen. The metal chairs and tables outside were bent in a way that suggested someone had tried to steal them too, possibly in hopes of residual coffee dust, but they were firmly bolted down.

The one usable set of chairs was currently occupied by Beau and Richena. They were leaned close together, looking like they were having an intense conversation, and I caught the words "storage bay." I slipped around to the side of the building, close enough to listen without being seen.

"It still smells like burnt coffee out here," Richena said. "Maybe it'll wake me up."

I inhaled deeply, wishing I could wrap the aroma around me and take it with me.

"Anyway," Beau said, "that Plutonian wasn't the first person to ask about the storage bay. You're taking a big risk."

"Thought that was your favorite thing about me." Her voice had a teasing sweetness. "And it's not like I'm doing anything wrong. It's not hurting anyone."

There was a moment's silence, and I peered around the corner and saw her slide her hand over his. I could almost feel the warmth of his hand from where I was watching. He said, "I know, but—"

"I'm going to catch that smuggler so I can get myself promoted. Then I'll get rid of all the bureaucracy and get something done with this stupid organization." That sounded like a good idea, until Richena went on. "I'll start by dumping all those rejects who got drafted into GUPPEAS for traffic accidents and criminal idiocy. And stop with ridiculous missions like rescuing some doctor who should have known better than to get herself into this mess. As far as I'm concerned, she can sit in a Plutonian dungeon forever."

Beau's tone was offended. "Fortunately, GUPPEAS doesn't agree with you there."

"Whatever," she said. I peeked around the corner again and saw they were getting up. "I'm going to take the shuttle out for a couple of hours before my ship's scheduled to take off."

"Cutting it a little close, aren't you?"

I didn't hear her reply. They walked back to where her ship was docked, and a few minutes later, a shuttle took off.

I lingered as the shuttlecraft grew smaller, and then I took another look at Richena's ship. I'd seen it before, at the GUPPEAS dock. It was newer than the *Turkey,* sleek and elegant, shaped like a long-necked dragon. There was a blank spot above the registration number on the hull. No doubt some committee was still deciding on a name.

Underneath the entry hatch, a uniformed Plutonian guard had nodded off, a cup of herbal tea precariously balanced on the arm of her chair. Apparently, she wasn't adjusting well to the caffeine ban. On her lap was the latest issue of *Inside Pluto Today,* with the front page hinting at some kind of scandal involving Queelchu, the Jupiter-an actress.

Nothing made any sense. What was Richena hiding? Why was Beau going along with it? What was I even doing on some planet that wasn't really a planet, trying to pretend I was a real spaceship captain?

Any other time, I would have had more sense. But I was exhausted from caffeine deprivation, my brain was moving at half speed, and I couldn't stop fixating on wanting to know Richena's secret. I slipped behind the guard without waking her, deactivated my gravity boots, and leaped up through the hatch into Richena's ship.

Once inside, I wasn't sure what to do next. I wanted to know what was in the locked storage bay, but I couldn't just grab someone and ask how to find it. I wandered up one corridor and down another, trying to look purposeful. A couple of times, I passed crew members, but they saw my GUPPEAS uniform and didn't pay me any mind. I wound up in front of a door with a bronze keypad inscribed, "Captain Richena R. R. Rossi."

The lock was probably a four-letter combination. I tried B-E-A-U. No luck. I tried R-R-R-R. Too obvious. There were a few million combinations.

I stared at my face, reflected in the keypad. I looked ridiculous in a uniform with a captain's insignia on the shoulder.

Wait.

The captain's insignia was what let me into my own quarters. I pressed it against the keypad, and the door slid open.

Richena's quarters were tastefully decorated in a blue so deep that it needed a fancy name like "azure" or "cerulean." A giant computer screen took up most of one wall, next to an aquarium filled with toothy black fish. The coffee table (can you still call it that with no coffee?) held a sketchbook of uniform designs, a perfectly plated tofu sandwich, and a copy of *Cosmological Magazine* opened to a quiz asking, *Is He the Right Anthropod for You?* ("When he sees an attractive woman walk by, does he (a) detach his eyestalk so I won't see him looking at her, (b) try to distract me by pretending that giant space ferrets are about to attack, or (c) offer to semi-marry us both?")

I stopped in front of the computer. Half the screen was filled with an unflattering picture of me grimacing over a plate of dried regel-worm at the ambassador's banquet. It took a moment to realize I was looking at the latest installment of Pietro's blog.

UPDATE FROM PLUTO!

I can now report that my ex, "Captain" Janet Delane, continues to wreak havoc wherever she goes. As soon as she arrived on Pluto, the government announced a ban on chocolate. Did Janet eat it all, or did she just stand next to a chocolate factory and cause it to explode, shooting all remaining traces of cocoa into the stratosphere?

Then, while Jam-it and her spectacularly incompetent crew were trying (and failing) to apprehend a chocolate smuggler, the Plutonians went ahead and banned coffee as well. So if you don't want to be condemned to a miserable existence on bread and water, stay away from Pluto—and away from Jam-it the Technology-Slayer.

I ground my teeth in fury. He had some nerve, blaming me for the chocolate and coffee bans. And no one but I had any business calling my crew incompetent.

I couldn't help myself: I kept reading.

Speaking of technology-slaying, it appears there have been no recent signs of life around the biggest fuelstone factory on Pluto. What's going on there, and what does it have to do with Janet? Check back soon.

That last part didn't make any sense. I scrolled down, but there was nothing else about it, just reader comments on how much they loved Pietro's stories, and several others alleging bizarre technological breakdowns that they wanted to blame on me, on planets I'd never visited. At the bottom, one of the reader comments caught my eye:

Pietro, it's obvious you want her back. Too bad she's probably found someone better by now.

Voices were approaching in the hallway, and one of them sounded like Richena's. How could she have returned so quickly? I dove into the closet, which was packed so full of clothes that I had to wrestle my way to the back to hide behind them. A moment later, the voices became clear as the door opened.

"I'll just be a minute," Richena was saying. Her high-heeled boots clicked along the floor, accompanied by another, heavier set of footsteps. "I should get back into uniform before we take off." She stopped at the closet door. I held my breath, trying not to move while becoming painfully aware that I was backed against a small metal object with a sharp corner.

"I should get going, then," Beau said.

"No hurry. Missions are always more fun when you're on board."

"Richena, we've been through this. I—"

There was a long silence.

Finally Beau said, "Not that I don't miss being kissed like that, but things didn't work out between us last time we were together. Or the time before that, or—"

"Careful; don't let anyone hear you say that." Richena walked to the closet and opened the door, inches away from me. "Which uniform do you think—the lilac or the avocado?"

"I can't believe GUPPEAS lets you get away with nonstandard uniforms. Have you seen what they make every other crew wear?"

"I'm sure they'll get around to issuing me a sternly worded letter, right after they come up with a name for my ship." She took hold of the uniform hanging directly in front of me, examined it, and let go so that it smacked me in the face. The metal corner behind me pressed hard into my back. Whatever it was, it was sitting on a pile of clothes at just the wrong height.

"Why don't you come up with a nickname for your ship? Captain Delane calls hers the *Turkey*. Though I'd have gone for something a little more spacey-sounding, like *Cosmic Turkey*."

"Oh, it's 'Captain Delane' now? Somehow, I don't think you were calling her that when you were tonguing her tonsils after the banquet. You know the Plutonians have to think we're still together. They believe in soulmates, and they'll never take you seriously as an ambassador if you can't even keep the peace in your own relationship."

"I realize that. I won't slip again. If I didn't know better, I'd think you were jealous of Janet."

"That space-opera wannabe? She's not your type." Richena fiddled in the closet for another moment, finally selecting a pale yellow uniform. "Guess I'll wear this one. Why did I join this ridiculous organization again?"

"As I recall, you were arrested for illegal possession of a—"

He was interrupted by another kiss, punctuated by encouraging noises from her. My stomach rolled itself into a ball and began pounding against my rib cage. When he finally managed to get her hooks out of him (or at least, that's the way I preferred to picture it), she said, "Admit it, Beau—you're a good boy, but you only like bad girls."

His voice was low, but I caught it. "It's true. I do."

She shut the closet door, muffling the rest of the conversation. I did hear when he said goodbye and left.

Richena stayed in her quarters while I felt the ship's engines start to fire up. Why didn't she go to the bridge so I could get out of here? If the ship took off with me still here, she'd find me and probably shove me out an airlock.

Richena sprayed on an aggressively authoritative-smelling perfume that made me want to sneeze. I pinched my nose and waited.

And waited.

I wasn't sure what Richena was doing. I couldn't hear anything; maybe she was reading Pietro's blog or sketching another uniform. Or maybe she knew I was here, and she'd decided to wait me out.

The perfume was like having a Saturnian flopperbird up my nose. I took a deep breath, tried to steady myself, and—

"Ah—CHOO!"

It was hopeless. I was caught. Richena would pull the closet open and I'd be permanently disgraced. I'd be arrested and—what did they do to arrestees when they'd already been forced to join GUPPEAS? Throw them in Exalted Leader's dungeons?

Nothing happened.

Nothing happened some more.

I felt a low vibration under my feet. The ship would be taking off within minutes.

I peeked out. No Richena.

I pushed the uniform aside and walked out into her empty quarters. The perfume smell was still there, but she was gone. The noisy high-heeled boots were sitting next to her bed, presumably replaced by sensible flats. The toothy fish all seemed to be grinning at me.

I looked back in the closet, grabbed the square metal object that had been annoying me, and carried it out into the light. It was an electronic datebook. Richena's appointments looked pretty mundane at first: lunch dates, hairdresser, GUPPEAS committee meetings. Something seemed off, but I couldn't put my finger on it.

The ship gave a lurch, and the datebook flew out of my hands, landing in the fish tank with a splash. The fish surrounded it, teeth snapping.

A computerized voice sounded: *"Three minutes to takeoff."*

A quick glance around the room yielded nothing that would protect me from getting my hand bitten off. Why couldn't Richena collect armored gloves or something? I took off my wide uniform sash and dropped a few pieces of Richena's tofu sandwich into the tank. The fish went straight for the food and devoured it so fast I barely had time to use my sash like a net to snare the datebook.

The sash snagged on the little plastic castle. One fish chomped down hard on the datebook, sash and all. I pulled at my end, but other fish were grabbing on to the sash, tearing at it.

The ship gave another lurch, and I bumped against the tank's environmental controls. There was a static noise, and the fish all went limp, eyes bulging.

I pulled the sash and datebook free. "You're not dead, are you? Please don't be dead."

One of the fish revived and swam to the edge of the tank to glare at me. Another woke and jumped above the water line, nearly escaping the tank.

"Oh good, it was just my technology hex. Bye."

"Two minutes to takeoff."

I fled the room and down the hallway, clutching the datebook and the dripping wet sash. Trying to find the most direct route to the main hatch, I passed a sealed door marked, "Absolutely no admittance, yes this DOES mean you, and you too!" I stopped. This had to be the shuttle bay with the mysterious contents.

"One minute to takeoff."

No time. I found the exit hatch and flung myself out of the ship.

The datebook fell from my pocket to the ground, and momentum landed me squarely on top of it, moments before the ship took off.

The Plutonian guard yawned, turned around to look at me, and said, "Wow, that perfume you're wearing is really aggressive." Then she picked up her newspaper.

Later, back in my own quarters, I examined Richena's appointment book for clues, but apparently the water had damaged it. Either that, or she had simultaneous appointments on different planets. "This doesn't make sense," I muttered. My technology-slaying curse had struck again.

I looked over at the current motivational poster, which showed a breathtaking view of an exotic purple mountain. At the bottom it said, *Climb every mountain: you might find your missing socks on top of one of them.*

"Not helping," I said.

Since we didn't have an engineer, I called Frink to see if he could fix the datebook.

"I'm a little busy dealing with a propulsion leak," Frink told me over the beepity-beeper.

"Propulsion leak? I thought everything was fixed."

"Nlubglub's blaming it on a Plutonian saboteur." Clanging and grinding noises nearly drowned him out. "I'll take a look at your datebook when I get the chance. Leave it on the desk in your quarters."

"I think I heard you wrong."

"Don't worry; I can get in. There should be a box marked 'Do Not Touch.' One of our old captains used to leave stuff in there for me. At least, I think that's why he left stuff in there." The call cut off.

The next day, I accompanied Beau to check on Pilar Villarreal in Plutonian custody. The guards escorted us to her laboratory in the basement of the compound. The room was cold enough to put goose-bumps all over me as soon as we walked in. (Or maybe it was the proximity to Beau.)

Pilar looked up from a handful of beakers when we walked in. "Thanks for coming. I'm researching a cure for Exalted Leader's caffeine allergy. Just my luck that curing the chocolate allergy made things worse. And to top it off, he's a bit of a meta-hypochondriac." Seeing our blank looks, she explained, "He has a pathological fear of developing a pathological fear of illness."

"Oh." I was shivering. "Maybe when you cure the caffeine allergy, you can convince him he has a secondary allergy to low temperatures?"

Beau elbowed me, causing my heart to flutter, which probably wasn't his intent. He said, "We're still looking for this smuggler. Is there anything you can tell us about her? How did you find her when you got the cupcake?"

"She found me." Pilar looked around, but the guards were across the room watching some sort of sport on the monitor. She dropped her voice. "It wasn't only the one cupcake."

"What do you mean?" I asked.

"She contacted me and asked if I would help her distribute chocolate as a public health measure."

I wasn't following this. "Public health?" I stole another glance at the guards, but they were raptly watching the monitor, where one team had just skewered the ball on a sword and thrown it into a flaming barrel.

"Public mental health," Pilar explained. "People need chocolate to keep them sane. Especially here on Pluto, where the rest of life is so dreary." She poured the contents of one beaker into another, and the red and green liquids started what appeared to be a fistfight.

"So when she contacted you," Beau said, "where did you meet her?"

"Near the big fuelstone processing plant on the other side of the planet, by the Great Frozen River. She told me there'd be no one around. Which is kind of weird. I mean, a busy factory like that, you'd think there'd be people going in and out all the time. But she was right."

The communications panel lit up with the image of Exalted Leader's face. "Progress report," he demanded.

"No progress yet, Your Exaltedness," Pilar said. "I'm sorry; these things take time."

The guards burst into cheers as their team threw the flaming barrel into a pile of feathers and mousetraps. Tiny mousetrap infernos were flying all over the arena onscreen.

Exalted Leader glanced at the score, then back at Pilar. "You'll cure this allergy, or I'll throw you back in the dungeon and have you tickled twice a day." He noticed Beau and me standing behind her. "And shouldn't you be out catching the smuggler?"

I was tempted to point out that he'd authorized this visit for us, but fortunately Beau spoke first. "Captain Rossi is pursuing some promising leads as we speak. And Dr. Villarreal is giving us information that may be helpful in tracking the smuggler down."

"I could always throw you all in the dungeon together." Exalted Leader's caffeine-deprived mood seemed to be getting steadily worse. "Guards! Escort these two out and make sure the doctor gets back to work." Two of the guards reluctantly tore themselves away from the game.

"Is there anything we can bring you?" I asked Pilar.

"Guards with better taste in entertainment?" She adjusted her glasses. "Just get me out of here. Soon."

The dream was too good to wake up from. Beau Dangere's voice was whispering in my ear, "I need to see you."

"Say that again," I purred.

My eyelids popped open. And I found that Beau Dangere was, in fact, talking to me through the beepity-beeper. "I need to see you," he whispered again.

"Why are we whispering?" I whispered back.

"I'll explain when we meet. How about that deserted place down the street from the capitol building, the one that used to be a coffee shop?"

I told him to give me an hour. After I hung up, I noticed that the rotating motivational poster in my quarters now had a picture of the pyramids and said: *Mindless obedience: the block that all successful organizations are built on.*

"Computer," I said, "I know you won't talk to me, but could you lose the motivational posters? They're annoying."

No response.

"At least get rid of the words. The pictures are okay."

The picture disappeared off the screen, and the words grew to a larger font.

"That counts as talking to me," I said.

"No, it doesn't," said a grating voice. Then the computer gasped with the realization of what it had done, and the screen went blank.

"Thanks," I said. "You know the computer on Richena Rossi's ship tells them when it's about to take off?"

I showered, put on a fresh uniform, and tried to figure out what to do with my hair. No amount of hairspray or mousse would keep it from going all over the place in the Plutonian gravity. I looked like I'd just stuck my finger in a light socket. I tried to squash the mop under my GUPPEAS-issued yellow beret.

On my way out, I passed Zeeko in the common room. "Captain," he said, "you should let me do something about your hair. It looks like you stuck your finger in a light socket."

"Why don't you go find the Plutonian saboteur?" I answered, and shoved my hat down harder on my head.

A moment later, I returned and said, "Sorry. Do what you can."

While Zeeko pinned my hair into place, I reminded myself that it was ridiculous to worry about what Beau thought of how I looked. He and Richena had to keep up appearances. No doubt Beau wanted to talk about some perfectly ordinary GUPPEAS-related business. At a deserted coffee shop. That he could only talk about in whispers.

When I got there, the ex-coffee shop looked worse than I

remembered. The walls were painted with graffiti in languages from several galaxies, and someone had made off with most of the bolted-down furniture, and the countertop as well. If they could have stolen the burnt-coffee smell, they'd probably have done that, but it was still there, fortunately. I sniffed nostalgically, dreaming of double espressos.

Beau motioned me to one of the two remaining outdoor seats and asked, "What do you know about that fuelstone factory that Dr. Villarreal mentioned?"

This was the urgent reason he had to see me? I cursed silently. "What does anyone know? Fuelstone is the number one industry on Pluto, and it's the reason GUPPEAS pretends Pluto is a real planet and tries to stay on friendly terms with that creepy Exalted Leader whose real name I've already forgotten."

"Fibbreous Nekwizzle. Anyway, my favorite blog also mentioned something about the factory, so I did some checking. It turns out no one's been seen around that building for the last two years, except the guards who bring the fuelstone out."

"I thought fuelstone was too volatile for a fully-automated factory."

"It is. There are parts of the process that have to be done manually." He leaned in, and I could smell his spicy aftershave mixed with burnt-coffee fumes. "And this is where it gets weird. Nobody's been seen taking the raw fuelstone ore inside. So where is the refined fuelstone coming from?"

I tried to piece this together. "Wasn't there a rumor a while back that Pluto was running out of fuelstone?"

"Supposedly. I assumed they'd started that story themselves to jack up the price. But they shut down most of the small factories after that big one opened."

"I think GUPPEAS will want to know about this." Which meant I'd have to find the form for reporting anomalous fuelstone situations, fill it out in triplicate, send it in, and hope for a response before the committees got reshuffled again. Unless Beau had a better idea.

"How about you and I go to the factory and do a little nosing around?"

Nosing around in a place I wasn't supposed to be, with an incredibly hot guy whose pretend girlfriend already hated me? "What about Richena?"

"I told her about it, and she didn't seem overly concerned. Besides, she's off chasing that smuggler."

This was going to get us into all kinds of trouble; I could feel it already. "Shouldn't we at least wait until night?"

"It is night in that part of Pluto."

"Oh." Why did his eyes have to be so gorgeous? "Okay."

He stood and reached out a hand to help me up. "Your hair looks good like that."

I caught my reflection in the broken shop window. In my committee-designed GUPPEAS uniform in clashing colors, my hair was the only thing about me that didn't look ridiculous. "Thanks."

We took Beau's floatcar to the other side of Pluto. I had time to check out the perks of an ambassador's vehicle: cloaking technology, massaging foot pedals, and cup holders inside the cup holders.

The cloaking technology kept us unseen while we hovered over the factory. A Plutonian ship parked outside was the only sign of life. "We should wait and see who belongs to that ship," he said. "It may be a while."

That was fine with me. We were less likely to get caught in a hidden floatcar than on the ground. I fumbled for a topic of conversation. I couldn't exactly ask him about the conversation I'd overheard with Richena. I noticed a book stuffed in one of the cup holders, and pulled it out.

"*Curling Not Hurling.*" I grinned. "Hey, is this any good? I think I have a copy."

"It's one of the best books on curling. Are you a fan of the sport?"

"Oh. Absolutely. I love curling. Practically born with..." I almost said *a curling stick*, before I remembered what it was. "...with a broom in my hand."

"Look!" Beau grabbed my arm and pointed.

A line of bored-looking Plutonians filed out with a load of containers. We waited for them to get to their ship, and then we climbed out of our invisible vehicle and slipped inside the building.

Inside the factory, the walls were shiny black, reflecting the rows of silver machines that reached from floor to ceiling. The sound of throbbing engines drowned out everything else except my nervous heartbeat. Beau pulled out a flashlight to examine the machines, and said something that was swallowed by the sound of gears and pistons cranking.

"What?"

He moved closer and said in my ear, "This doesn't look like fuelstone."

"Doesn't smell like fuelstone either." There was an oily smell, but not the familiar burnt-rubber stench.

The machines were bumping and grinding, but no one was there to run them, not even a misplaced robot. Aisle upon aisle of machines cranked out nothing but Plutonian tourist tchotchkes. Key chains with pictures of Exalted Leader. Snow globes with models of Exalted Leader's palace. And t-shirts, piles of t-shirts. *Someone on Pluto loves me. I heart Pluto, Realest of the Real Planets. My clone went to Pluto and all I got was a copy of this t-shirt.* Two-armed, four-armed, and tentacled versions. They even had a no-armed one, presumably for Jupiterans. I'm guessing that one didn't sell well, but the machine cranked out mountains of them.

Beau chuckled as he held up a picture frame shaped like one of the toothy fish I'd seen in Richena's quarters. "Wedding souvenirs."

"Fish get married on Pluto?"

"Not that I know of. The Plutonian wedding custom is for the couple to balance as many fish as they can on each other's heads. It symbolizes…actually, I have no idea what it symbolizes." He put the frame back.

I said, "Pluto's not really my idea of a romantic wedding spot."

"Mine either. I'd go more for one of the planets around Fornax."

That was exactly my idea of a perfect place for a wedding, with lush vegetation and a golden sky. Richena could have Pluto. I could picture her with fish on her head, balanced on top of that immovable knot of auburn hair.

We searched up one aisle and down another. "Are you sure this is the right place?" I asked.

"I am. Well, I was." Beau leaned on one of the machines. "I'd do anything for a cup of decent coffee right about now."

"Good to know," I said.

He gave me a grin that made me blush, then turned the flashlight on the nearest door. "Let's keep looking."

Two hours and several thousand tentacle-friendly tote bags later, we found a quiet corridor that ended in a door with a conspicuous lock. "Somebody's been here," I said, which was probably unnecessary given the footprints in the dust around the door. "Somehow, I don't think there's going to be a key hidden on the doorframe."

"Do you think a Jupiteran could get through the keyhole?" he suggested.

"Probably not." I rattled the door and tried to think. What would a decent burglar like Frink do in a situation like this?

He'd use the electronic lockpick.

Which was still in my pocket.

I pulled it out. It had been through the laundry a couple of times, but it lit up when I pushed the button. I pressed it against the lock, and the door slid open.

Beau grinned. "You have a lockpick?"

"Sure." I tried to sound casual. Beau liked bad girls, right? "I always carry one."

He shined the flashlight into the room.

A machine nearly filled the entire room, with an assortment of wheels, pulleys, panels, and spinning lights in eight different colors. The lights looked like what would happen if a disco ball got drunk. The machine emitted a low throbbing hum, occasionally punctuated with a sound like a cow falling onto a pile of bicycle horns.

"Any idea what this is?" Beau asked.

"Not a clue."

"We need your ship's engineer."

"I don't have one," I said.

"Really?"

"Really." I looked the machine up and down again. The humming changed to a quicker tempo. "But I know where we can get one. I'll call Martian."

I waited for Beau to say that there are no Martians. He didn't. This was the final proof that he was the perfect man.

I used the beepity-beeper to call my brother, who picked up right away. "Hey, Janet. I was just talking to Mom, and she wanted to know what the deal was with Pietro's latest blog post."

"I have no idea." I'd managed to resist reading him since that day in Richena's quarters, and I wasn't keen on discussing Pietro in front of Beau. I gave Martian a short version of how we'd wound up in the factory. "We've discovered this strange machine that the Plutonians are trying to keep secret. Beau—I mean, Ambassador Dangere—asked me to find an engineer to discreetly look it over."

"Cool. Did you find one?"

I waited.

"Oh. I get it. But the thing is, that Exalted Leader guy isn't allowing any aliens on the planet except the ones from GUPPEAS. Something about being afraid they're smuggling coffee. What's up with that?"

"Just take a look and tell me what you think." I turned the camera portion of the beepity-beeper toward the machine. Martian gasped. When I looked back at the screen, he was wearing the expression of someone who'd just seen God.

"What is it?" I asked him.

"I don't know. But I'm joining GUPPEAS, and I'll be there as soon as I can."

6

Not With Walnuts

A few days later, I was summoned to the dank basement room that Vertin Bogler was using as an office during his visit to Pluto. His aura was such a pale green today, I could barely make out his face, but his voice still sounded like that of a used-spaceship salesman who wants to offer you a super deal while they last. "New orders came in for you, since Captain Rossi has taken over the search for the smuggler."

New orders, taking me away from Pluto? I thought of Martian, and how much he wanted to see that machine. And the way Beau had smiled at me when I pulled out the lockpick.

Then I thought of the chance to be off this freezing non-planet where I couldn't have coffee, tea, or chocolate. "What's the assignment?"

"I had the papers here a minute ago. Now, where did I leave them?" He shuffled through the pile of paperwork on his desk.

One of Exalted Leader's officers came storming in. I didn't know her name, but I recognized her assortment of medals, all crowded onto the left side of her uniform. "This is outrageous!" she shouted.

"Of course it is," Bogler said soothingly. "Could you be a bit more specific?"

"The smuggler filled an entire town's water supply with café mocha. And somehow managed to escape."

My heart leapt. My mouth watered. "What town was this?"

"Exalted Leaderville."

"Over by the Great Frozen River?" Bogler asked.

"No, you're thinking of Exalted Leaderburg. Exalted Leaderville is about an hour from here."

"I'm sure Captain Rossi will be right on it," Bogler said.

The Plutonian's antennae pointed straight at him. "Your organization has failed to apprehend the smuggler. And your Dr. Villarreal must know more than she is telling. If this continues, she should be subjected to Saturnian appendix torture."

I wasn't sure what that meant, but Bogler's aura turned an alarming bright green. Bright enough that I spotted a page on the corner of his desk: *New assignment for Captain Delane and crew: opening negotiations with giant space squid on Alcyone 4.* I scanned the next few lines. *The previous 3 parties sent on this mission have not returned.* Someone, probably Bogler, had added a handwritten note in the margin: *Probably best not to mention this part to Cptn. Delane.*

While Bogler and the Plutonian were distracted with geography, I stuffed the assignment papers under my hat and patted it back into place. "This smuggler is very devious," I said. "My crew could provide backup for Captain Rossi. We could help with, you know, collecting evidence or something."

Bogler looked relieved. Maybe he didn't care for the idea of sending me to deal with giant space squid either. "Excellent idea, Captain. You and your crew should go there right away."

We arrived late at Exalted Leaderville, after Frink got it mixed up with Exalted Leader Village. By the time we landed and exited the ship, the reservoir was already full of clear, sparkling water. Some sharp-toothed fish, similar to the ones in Richena's aquarium, were zooming around at breakneck speed. One of them kept trying to climb up the bank, then slipping back down.

"The fish are still really hyper," the town's mayor told us, "but otherwise everything is under control. We drained and replaced the water as soon as Exalted Leader contacted us." He sounded disappointed.

"You drained it to where, exactly?" Lola's aura brightened with the question. I'd brought her and Frink, figuring Zeeko wouldn't be much help and Nlubglub would probably start a fight about the billiard riots with the nearest Plutonian.

"Oh, you know. There." The mayor gestured vaguely, avoiding eye contact. "Into the soil." His antennae started shaking, as if he'd had a lot of caffeine recently.

I tried to sound professional. "Did anyone see where the mocha came from?"

"Witnesses saw a small vessel, maybe sized for one person. The smuggler was quick. But I told all this to Captain Rossi." He pointed to a group of about twenty people, Plutonian and otherwise, at the far side of the reservoir. "She's over there, talking to reporters."

"Of course she is." I could see that knot of hair in the center of the crowd, with Beau standing next to her. And then I saw something else. A distinctive glow, a shade of purple that only matched one Venusian aura that I knew.

Pietro.

"Excuse me a moment." I stepped away, sat down on a rock near the reservoir, and checked my beepity-beeper. Pietro's blog had flashing lights and mock sirens, as if he were breaking an important news story.

EXCLUSIVE! COFFEE AND CHOCOLATE CAPER ON THE COLDEST PLANET!

As faithful readers know, Pluto currently has a ban on everything with caffeine, including chocolate. The residents of Exalted Leaderville pretended not to be cheering when a rogue ship appeared next to their reservoir and infused it with a perfectly mixed concoction of café mocha. (Seriously, mocha? Those have been passé on every civilized planet since the invention of the ionized coffee-nitrogen shot. Plutonians probably think wobblefruit toast is a hip new creation.)

Witnesses report that the individual who spiked the water appeared humanoid, possibly female, and did not have a uniform matching any known space-faring organization. Many of the locals were seen diving into the reservoir and imbibing heavily. They assured me afterward that they were just trying to dispose of the contraband so no one would be tempted by it.

The smuggler left just in time to be pursued by the charming, elegant captain assigned by GUPPEAS, Janet Delane. Just kidding! The elegant captain in question was Richena Rossi, who chased the smuggler halfway to Jupiter before losing sight of the ship in an asteroid field. Yours truly will be publishing an exclusive interview with Captain Rossi and her fiancé, Ambassador Beau Dangere. Check back soon!

Fiancé?

A loud splash made me look up. One of the fish had made an impressive attempt to escape the water, just in time for me to see Pietro coming toward me with Richena and Beau. I switched my beepity-beeper away from his blog, back to an official GUPPEAS channel.

"Janet." Pietro's voice was too perky for someone on a caffeine-free planet. "I was hoping I'd run into you."

"Pietro." I twitched an attempt at a smile. "What brings you here?" And was I imagining it, or had his eyes changed from their normal gold to brown? I'd never seen that before.

"Reporting on the story for *Primarily Pietro*, of course. My readers are going to love this."

"Oh, you're still doing the blog?" I said, with the airy tone of someone who's moved on to bigger and better things. "Well, it's good that you're branching out. Last time I saw it, your blog only had two topics: yourself and me."

Beau chuckled. "You have to admit, Captain Delane has a point."

Pietro's smile didn't change, but his aura fizzled for a moment. "Actually, starting next week, it's no longer a blog." There it was again: his eyes turned lavender. *"Primarily Pietro* has been picked up as a weekly column for the *Galactic Times*, in the Nonhuman Interest section."

"The *Galactic Times?*" I blurted. "You've got to be kidding."
Reporters spent their whole careers trying to get into the *Times*, the
most popular newspaper in the Milky Way.

Pietro's brightening aura spread so far, I took a step back to avoid
the purple glow. He smirked. "Not bad, huh? They recognize talent
when they see it. My audition for them was a story about a tragic
prom night and the romantic dreams that might have been but were
ruined by someone's technology hex and dancing the Ditzy Space
Owl."

All the humiliation from that night rushed back. I wanted to climb
inside the nearest rocket and shoot myself to the other side of the
universe.

Lola came up the path toward us. Pietro was a little too obvious
about looking her over. "Hello," he said. "Who are you?"

I wished I could stuff one of those fish into his leering face.

Lola ignored him and gave me a formal salute, the first time I'd
ever seen her do that. "Any orders, Captain?"

I saluted back and tried to think of a response that sounded like
something a real captain would say. "We'll discuss that after we have
all the information." I turned to Richena. "We're providing your backup. Any indication of where the smuggler was headed next?"

"If I knew that, we wouldn't be standing here." Richena's voice
could have frozen the reservoir. "There is one thing you could do that
would be a big help."

"What's that?" I hoped it wouldn't involve giant space squid.

"My crew was supposed to play a curling match tomorrow
against the local Plutonian team. One of those goodwill things. Your
crew can take care of that, so mine is free to do the real work."

"Curling?"

"Curling should be all right," Pietro said. "A broom isn't too technological for Janet." His eyes turned beige.

I had to ask. "Did your eyes just change color?"

"What?" Pietro's eyes turned pink. "Oh, the lenses." He removed
them, showing the golden eyeballs underneath, the ones I used to
stare at lovingly. "They're the latest—"

"They were a fad on Venus," Lola interrupted, "a couple of years ago. I didn't think anyone used them anymore."

Pietro's aura faded a bit. "Sometimes it's fun to be retro," he said. "But I should probably leave them off, since they might explode with Janet here. Anyway, since no one seems to be busy chasing smugglers right now, maybe Captain Rossi and her fiancé have time for that interview they promised?"

Beau's eyes widened. "We're not actually—"

"Now would be the perfect time," Richena said. She took Pietro's arm on one side and Beau's on the other, leading them back toward where Frink was talking to the mayor. "Be sure to send us a video of the curling match," she called over her shoulder.

"Good," Lola said, loud enough for them to hear. "We won't have any distractions while we discuss strategy for catching the smuggler." Under her breath, she added, "Guys like him are the worst. I hope Frink steals those stupid lenses."

It was weird having Lola back me up, but I wasn't complaining. At least I'd maintained my captain-like dignity in front of Pietro and Richena and, most importantly, Beau.

Lola said, "There's a fish on your leg."

I looked down to see a football-sized fish chomp hard on my ankle.

Most of Pluto heard me scream as I jumped three feet in the air.

The curling match was played on the same reservoir, now mocha-free and frozen overnight by turning off some of the heating devices that normally made it bearable to be outdoors on Pluto. A target had been drawn on the ice, with concentric rings in red, white, and blue. I could see the fish swimming underneath, chomping those giant mouths. Temporary bleachers had been set up, and were slowly filling with spectators.

Lola, Frink, and Zeeko arrived with brooms. Lola took one look at Zeeko and yanked his broom away. "Not a chance," she said. She handed the broom to me. "We need four players, so you're in."

"Me? But you've all played before. You, Frink, Nlubglub, Zeeko—that's four."

"Last time, Zeeko swept in the wrong direction," Frink said.

"It's true." Zeeko chuckled. "Nlubglub had to stop Lola from smacking me with a broom."

I looked at Nlubglub. "Where's your broom?"

"I've got that covered." Nlubglub sprouted a broom-shaped limb. "Anyway, trust us, we're better off with you playing. You've read *Curling Not Hurling*, right?"

"Sure." I'd read the first chapter before the pain from the fish bite became too distracting. The gist was that one player took a rock the size of a flattened bowling ball, and slid it along the ice from the starting line toward the target. The other players used brooms to sweep a path in front of the rock to get it to the position they wanted. "How hard could it be?"

The Plutonian team arrived. They were all twice my size, with personalized rocks and 6-speed brooms.

"Mechanical brooms? That's cheating." Frink's eyes turned from orange to gray. "Also, I want one."

The Plutonian team captain gave me a smug look, antennae straight up. "Intergalactic rules don't specify a type of broom."

"That's correct," said the mayor, who was acting as umpire for the occasion.

I spotted Beau hurrying down from the stands, heading toward us. Bad enough that I had to make a complete fool of myself playing a game I knew nothing about. I had to embarrass myself in front of Beau too?

Beau pulled me aside, his face creased with worry. "Exalted Leader is upset this morning. First there was some sort of holdup in fuelstone production, and then Dr. Villarreal's latest attempt at a cure didn't work. He ordered her sent to work in a fuelstone mine."

That sentence would be awful enough for a Plutonian, and they were accustomed to the cold. For a human, it could prove deadly. "He can't do that. Can he?"

"I tried everything to talk him out of it. Finally, I convinced him that coming to the curling match would improve his mood. He said he'll let Dr. Villarreal stay here and keep working on a cure for his allergy. But only if the GUPPEAS team wins."

My stomach sank. "Do we even have a chance?"

"It'll be all right." Beau gave the kind of smile that banishes darkness in whole galaxies. "I'm the five-time curling champion for GUPPEAS."

One of the Plutonian curlers looked over from a few yards away and sauntered toward us, whistling some terrible Betelgeusean pop song.

"Thank goodness, because I have no idea what I'm doing," I said. Not that this was any different from any other day since I'd joined GUPPEAS.

The Plutonian curler started making practice moves with her broom, sliding closer to us.

"And the winning team gets a cup of coffee." Beau held up a hand. "Not a cup apiece. Just one cup to share."

The Plutonian curler was carefully not looking at us, but her antennae were cocked in our direction. Something wasn't right. I looked straight at her. "What are you doing?"

She flicked a switch on her broom and shoved it toward us. The ice beneath us started to crack. Beau pushed me back just in time; then he disappeared beneath the freezing water.

A crowd came racing over, including my crew. Nlubglub stretched two limbs into the water and pulled out a shivering Beau. His teeth were chattering, and the water soaking his uniform was rapidly crystallizing into ice.

"Blankets!" I yelled. "We need a medic, now!"

Within moments, Beau was wrapped in blankets and loaded onto a hover-gurney. They whisked him away for medical care.

"So sorry." The Plutonian player's voice dripped with sincerity. "Broom malfunction. I've never seen that happen before."

"Oh, come on," I said, but was drowned out by Plutonians loudly commiserating that yes, it was a terribly unfortunate accident. A smirking Pietro took pictures of the hole in the ice, and of me.

The mayor/umpire marched over, jowls flopping. "Exalted Leader is tired of waiting. Refreeze that spot, and let's get the game started."

"Are you kidding?" I tried to get up in the mayor's face, but I barely reached his collar. "We need to see if the ambassador is all right."

"He'll be fine. But you won't be, if you keep Exalted Leader waiting."

"But Beau is on the team."

"Do you have four people who can play?"

"What if we don't?"

"Then you forfeit the game now, and your Earth doctor goes to work in the fuelstone mines."

Lola grabbed my arm. "We have four players. C'mon, Captain." She steered me toward the starting line and set a flat-bottomed stone in front of me.

I slid the heavy stone onto the ice. It didn't get far until Frink and Nlubglub ran ahead. Nlubglub shape-shifted into a broom and, together with Frink, swept a path that put the stone just inches away from the center of the target.

"Foul!" "You can't do that!" "Cheat!" The Plutonians pointed at Nlubglub in a sputtering rage.

Nlubglub slid back into their regular shape. "Intergalactic rules don't specify a type of broom."

After a brief, loud antennae-wrestle with the mayor, the Plutonian captain stalked to the starting line and positioned his stone. He slid it, his teammates swept, and his stone knocked mine off the target, clear to the edge of the reservoir.

"But—but—" I looked from one crew member's face to another. "Can they do that?"

"Of course," Lola said. "Do you even know how this game works?"

I gave her a look so empty, it could have been a black hole.

Zeeko leaned over from where he was sitting with the spectators.

"After each round of play, which is called an end, the team with the rock closest to the center of the target gets a point for every rock that's closer to the center than the other team's nearest stone. But only if they're inside the target, so your last one isn't much help."

My first attempts at sweeping weren't great. Partly because Zeeko kept trying to help with shouted instructions. "Left, no, your other left, no, your *other* other left! Wait, no, right!" It got better after Lola shoved him back into the stands and threatened to cram a broom down his throat if he didn't shut up.

A purple glow in the audience irritated the corner of my eye. Pietro was filming, and his aura was at his most cheerful violet.

My crew members were decent players, and I tried to copy their moves. We fumbled through the game, sliding, sweeping, strategizing positions, and I started to understand why curling is nicknamed "chess on ice." We went from twelve points behind to dead even. Then we reached the tenth end.

One after another, the Plutonians knocked our stones out of the way, landing their own squarely inside the house. Their eighth stone landed dead center. There were gasps from the crowd. "A perfect eight-ender!"

Lola set down the final rock. "No pressure," Frink told her. "All we have to do is knock theirs off the center and make sure yours lands closer than any of the other ones." He tossed me a broom.

She slid the rock, and we started to sweep. A low electrical hum came from Frink's broom. How did he have one of the mechanical ones?

I glanced over at Frink. He winked a purple eye at me.

The lenses went from purple to solid black, and Frink stumbled around blindly. Flames shot out of the bottom of his broom. I grabbed the broom away from him. Which button stopped the flames? I pushed one at random.

The broom flew from my hands, still spewing fire, and landed on the target. The ice collapsed underneath it, and eight stones and the broom crashed into the water.

One small piece of the target's outer edge remained on the ice.

And that was where Lola's stone, swept by Nlubglub, came to rest.

The mayor walked over and looked down into the water, bewildered. The fish had already swarmed in and torn the stones to pieces. He looked over at Exalted Leader, who nodded. "One point to the GUPPEAS team," the mayor said. "GUPPEAS wins."

The Plutonian team stormed over, cursing and screaming that we were cheats. Nlubglub stretched tall enough to look down on them, sprouting fists all over. "Who are you calling cheats? The broom never touched any of the rocks."

"And annihilating the target isn't cheating?"

My beepity-beeper sounded. Probably a good time to ignore it and get things calmed down here.

It was Beau.

I backed away from the noisy argument and answered the call. Beau was in a hospital bed, wrapped in a foil blanket. He was still shivering, but his smile was all warmth. "Nice play there, Captain. You're probably on every viewscreen on Pluto right now."

"Are you okay?"

"He'll be home in no time." Pilar Villarreal moved next to him. "And thanks for keeping me out of the fuelstone mines. For today, anyway."

"We'll get you home." I tried to sound more confident than I felt. "Hang in there a little longer."

"Oh, I'm fine. Not going stir crazy." Her smile was slightly off. "Except for drawing the molecular breakdown of chocolate all over the walls of my cell. And that guard who thought he overheard me getting into an argument with a table? He was completely mistaken."

Beau gave her a concerned look. "I know this is really rough on you, Doc, being stuck here. Don't give up."

Her voice quavered. "I've started liking Plutonian reality shows. Even the dating ones. I can't believe Gurfel picked Nimthit over Zessla."

"I kind of liked Nimthit," Beau said.

She gave him a scorching look. "That's what the table said."

I did the only helpful thing I could think of: I sent a text message to Vertin Bogler. *You know that cup of coffee we were supposed to get for winning the curling match? Please send it to Beau Dangere and Dr. Villarreal.*

A moment later, he texted back. *Sure. Also, some Martian just got here and says he's assigned to your ship. I thought there were no Martians?*

I looked back at Beau on the screen. "My engineer's here, so we can look into that, um, other matter as soon as you're feeling better." Probably best not to mention the fuelstone factory when I wasn't sure who might be listening.

Beau nodded understanding. "I'll be out tomorrow morning. Right, Doc?"

"As long as you don't mention Nimthit again."

I disconnected and looked up, just in time for a broom to whiz past my head. I'd forgotten about the argument, which was on the verge of turning into a full-fledged brawl. Nlubglub and the Plutonians were screaming at each other about last year's billiard riots. Zeeko was on the ground, being punched by a fish. Frink's eyes were back to their normal orange, and he appeared to be holding Lola and a Plutonian apart, but he was really grabbing their wallets.

"Hey!" I yelled loudly enough to get everyone's attention. "We're a peace organization, remember? Everyone in my crew, back to the ship. Now. That's an order."

Lola shot an angry look in my direction, but backed away from the Plutonians and headed for the docking bay. Frink helped Zeeko to his feet, and they followed.

A Plutonian swung a fist at Nlubglub, who grabbed him by the arm and held him a few inches off the ground. "I'm Jupiteran. There's nothing much you can do that will hurt me except give me a brainache with your stupidity. Now give it a rest before I accidentally drop you on top of those hungry fish." Nlubglub set down the Plutonian, not gently, and joined us.

Frink was walking with an odd, stiff-legged gait. I sighed. "You're hiding one of those brooms in your pants, aren't you?"

"Just don't walk too close. I don't want it to burn my toes off." He rubbed his eyes. "These lenses are really itchy. I should sneak them back into Pietro's pocket."

My beepity-beeper chirped a notification. I looked down to see a new post on Pietro's blog, topped by a picture of me looking terrified with a flame-shooting broom in my hand.

Later that day, Nlubglub opened the hatch and Martian strolled onto the bridge of the *Turkey.* He managed to hug me and salute at the same time.

"You're almost cute," Lola said. "Are you sure you're an engineer?"

I stepped back and grinned at him in his ridiculous GUPPEAS uniform. His dark hair had grown back thick and wavy after the hands-free razor incident. Like me, he was pale from spending too much time working in the edible-air factory. Unlike me, he didn't have to stand on tiptoe to look the rest of the crew in the eye. He was a year younger than I was, but had graduated a year earlier, after reprogramming the school's computers to change all the test answers to puns on the teachers' names.

"Thanks for coming," I said.

"No problem. The managers were threatening to fire me anyway."

"They caught you adding unnecessary features to the equipment again?"

"Depends on what you mean by 'unnecessary.' The portable snack synthesizer came in handy when I got hungry on the night shift." He ran a hand through his hair, and I noticed tiny dots of blue dye on his neck and hands. "I guess the detachable electric blunderbuss built into the light fixture was unnecessary, but it was really cool."

"So what took you so long?" I asked.

"I had to figure out what kind of crime to commit, and then get the engineering done to pull it off. I didn't want to go with something that had been done before, like shaving an obscene message into the mayor's pet ocelot."

"Or putting a hole in the side of City Hall?" Lola added drily, looking at me.

"Do you have to commit a crime to join GUPPEAS?" Zeeko asked. "I think I joined just because I felt like it."

Martian walked over to the computer, where he pulled up a diagram of our hometown. "I started by reprogramming the showers for the edible-air factory managers and board members—here, here, and here." He lit up locations while an ad for liquid furniture ran along the bottom of the screen. "I used a harmless dye to turn everyone blue for the next month or so."

Nlubglub stretched taller to get a look. "Should've gone with purple."

"When they hit the emergency broadcast system, they discovered I'd rewired it to play the worst country-western song ever: 'You've Made the Down Payment but You Haven't Signed the Mortgage on My Heart.' And also rigged the blunderbuss to spray candied walnuts all over the side of the factory in the shape of the mayor's pet ocelot, with an obscene message on its back."

I shook my head slowly. "I'm guessing that hasn't been done before."

"Not with walnuts." Martian beamed back at me. "And I candied them in a new machine I made out of the remains of your old float-car."

"Okay," Frink said, "he's an engineer, all right."

An unfamiliar voice, creaky from disuse, said, "It's about time."

I looked around. "Who was that? The Plutonian saboteur?"

"No," Martian said, "that was the computer."

I looked from him to the console and back. "But it never talks."

"I never had anyone I wanted to talk to," the computer answered. "Only engineers understand me."

Martian touched the console reverently. I think it purred.

This time Beau and I took the whole crew with us to the fuelstone factory. We used his floatcar again, since the *Turkey* didn't have cloaking technology. I tried to think of a tactful way to ask him about being referred to as Richena's fiancé. "So, how did the interview go with Pietro?"

"I wouldn't really call it an interview," Beau said. "He did most of the talking."

Lola snorted. "Imagine my surprise."

"Yeah, that sounds like Pietro," Martian said, looking up from a control panel. We zipped unseen past a patrol ship. "Your cloaking technology is impressive. Why doesn't the *Turkey* have anything like this?"

"Not compatible with the computer," Frink said. "Maybe you can get the computer to tell you what is compatible with it?"

We landed in front of the deserted factory, only to find the door sealed shut.

I pulled out the electronic lockpick. Trying to look casual, as if I did this all the time, I smiled coolly at Beau and pressed it against the lock.

The lockpick made a sputtering noise and shut itself off.

Frink held out his hand. I sighed and gave him back his lockpick. He made a couple of adjustments, tried again, and the door slid open. We all hurried inside. "I don't know how you do that, Captain. It was working fine before."

"Electronic lockpick?" Martian yelled over the noise of the machines. "Aren't those illegal?"

"Can't hear you!" Frink yelled back. "Hey, Nlubglub, did you see these anti-Jupiteran t-shirts?" He held up one that said *Jupiter Rhymes With Stupider.* This unleashed a torrent of squeaky outrage from Nlubglub, which killed any attempt at further discussion.

We'd brought flashlights, except for Lola, whose pink aura generated enough light for her to find her way around. We walked past the factory equipment, which was still spewing out tourist knickknacks, though it looked like no one was bothering to collect them. Not much point when Pluto wasn't getting any tourists. "I could use some of these machine parts to make a really sweet jet pack," Martian said.

"Forget it," I told him. "And, Frink, whatever you just stuffed in your pockets, put it back." He was two rows away, but I figured it was a good guess.

"Yes, ma'am," Frink said.

"And that includes anything you put in your boots, your hat, or anywhere else."

I noticed the coffee-mug machine had been repurposed to make hats with holes for Saturnian antennae. Beau held one up to show me the logo: "I Left All 3 of My Hearts on Pluto." He grinned, and I thought of the perfect witty response, then promptly forgot it when one of the machines went silent.

"What happened?" I called.

"Just doing an upgrade!" Nlubglub yelled back.

I walked over. Nlubglub was still by the machine with the anti-Jupiteran shirts, reprogramming it to print, "Pluto: Not Even a Real Planet."

"You realize no one's supposed to know we were here, right?" I said. "And that you're the security chief?"

Nlubglub grumbled and disabled the machine altogether. "It'll look like an accident."

Beau led us through the maze of the factory, until we both recognized the inner door. This time, though, it had obviously been reinforced.

Frink tried the electronic lockpick first, without success.

"Let me see that," Martian said. He pried the tiny device open. "It's working. Cool contraption, by the way."

I tried the door again. "If it's working, why can't we get in?"

Nlubglub pointed. "They've added a manual lock."

"No problem." Frink pulled out a bit of gold wire, which looked suspiciously like the hair ornament Lola had been wearing earlier. Lola glared.

"Think positive thoughts," Frink told her. "Otherwise, your aura gets so dark I can't see."

"Think about smacking him upside the head or something," Zeeko suggested pleasantly.

Lola's aura got so bright that I suspected she was thinking about smacking them both. But Frink still couldn't get the lock open. He gave up, and Lola snatched the wire out of his hand.

I was stymied. "We'll need a battering ram or something."

"In this gravity?" Lola shook her head, curls floating on the air. "That would barely nudge the door. We need explosives."

The door swung open, and we stood face-to-face with two very surprised guards.

"Quick!" I yelled at them, pointing down the hall. "Get out, before Exalted Leader finds out you let intruders in!"

My brazenness confused them for a fraction of a second, long enough for Lola to grab one guard and Nlubglub the other, and slam the two of them together. The guards were knocked unconscious and started floating away down the hall.

Martian saw the machine. His face contorted in wonder, breath coming fast. He dropped to his knees and gazed rapturously.

I hated to cut through the moment. "Do you know what it is?"

"No. But I'm going to find out."

And then he was examining, tweaking, taking measurements, opening up panels to peer inside. The rest of us quickly gave up asking questions and just handed him tools when he asked. Finally, he stopped and pointed. "I'm pretty sure this button operates it, but I'm still trying to figure out its exact function. Maybe we should—"

The room went black.

And then, not.

7

Plan Indeterminate Symbol

We were spinning, whirling, with white lights on every side splitting apart into multicolored prisms.

"Zeeko," I said with surprising calm, "you pushed the button, didn't you?"

"I sort of fell into it."

The words sounded stretched out, distorted, and now it felt like my body was distorting too, as if the atoms had too much space between them.

We landed with a crash on something solid and cold. No machine, no building, no walls around us, the light a confusion of different colors. Next to me was a purple mass, circles and trapezoids intersecting like a geometry lesson gone horribly wrong. It groaned and started to shape-shift. Nlubglub.

We were outdoors, on an endless, winding path of solid ice, with trees on either side. The multicolored lights turned out to be Lola's aura, which had turned a garish plaid. Beau helped Frink to his feet, then offered a hand to Zeeko, who just stared at it. I pulled myself up and looked around. "Where's Martian?"

"Whoa!" Martian came running from behind the trees. "Where do you think we are?"

Beau slipped, then righted himself. "The Great Frozen River?"

"No, we're not on Pluto." Frink studied the night sky. "The gravity's Earth-like, and the constellations are all wrong." Above us spread a starry sky with four moons visible, three green and one blue. In the tinted moonlight, I could see cactus plants and tall pine-like trees beside the ice, with clumps of needles at the end of each branch. The soft buzz of machinery came from everywhere at once.

Martian laughed like a child with a new toy. "It's a planar dislocator. I've never seen one before, much less used it."

"A plane what?" Lola asked. Her aura was slowly resolving into its normal pinkish hue. Next to her, Nlubglub flowed back into the shape of a rubber ball with legs.

"A planar dislocator." Martian's face was flushed with excitement, or maybe it was just the cold. "It transports matter to a predetermined spot. Theoretically, it can go any distance. We could be in another galaxy."

"Another galaxy?" I reached for my beepity-beeper, but it was silent on every channel. "There's no way to get home?"

"Sure, we can get home," Martian said. "We just need to get the planar dislocator to work in reverse."

"And how do we do that, when it's on Pluto and we're here?"

"Um. That might be a problem."

Nlubglub stretched to three meters tall and looked over the trees. "If we're not on Pluto, why are we on the Great Frozen River?" No one had a good answer to that. "And why are we standing on a big red-and-blue target symbol?" Nobody had an answer for that one either, but it seemed like a good idea to move to the riverbank.

I took one step and fell flat on my face.

"You forgot to turn off the gravity function on the boots," Beau said, helping me up. He bent down and pulled the lever on my boot rim so that I could walk normally. His hand brushed against my leg, and I nearly fell over again.

Behind the foliage, we found the source of the whirring noise: a series of waist-high machines that lined the river for as far as we could see in both directions. Martian examined one. "Portable weather-control device. Kind of an old model."

Beau looked back at the river. "It's a replica. Who would bother to recreate Pluto's entire Great Frozen River?"

"Plutonians?" Zeeko suggested helpfully.

There was a blinding flash of beige light, and we had just enough time to duck into the underbrush before two forms materialized on the target. The guards from the factory.

"They must have come here," the male guard said. "Last place we saw them was in the room with the planar thingamajig."

I stayed very still. My fingers dug into Martian's arm, because he wanted to tell them all about the planar dislocator. I knew my brother.

The female guard peered at the trees. Her gaze slid right past where I was hiding. "We should have waited for the reinforcements. When are they getting here?"

"How should I know? You're the one who called them."

Her antennae stood very straight. "I told you to do it."

"I thought you said—oh, no." He sat down on a rock, barely an arm's length away from me. "Someone's going to show up eventually, right?"

"I don't know. Whenever they need the next delivery. Could be weeks." She sat next to him. "I'm kinda woozy from getting my head knocked. How many intruders were there? Was that a human or a Saturnian?"

"I thought there was a Jupiteran, but that can't be right. A Jupiteran wouldn't be on Pluto." He yawned and stretched. From behind a bush, Frink reached over and deftly removed his watch. "I'm not feeling too good either. Let's rest here for a minute."

"Do you read that blog *Primarily Pietro*?" the woman asked.

Pietro? Seriously? My nails dug into my palms. I didn't even know what planet I was on, and I still had to hear about Pietro?

"Once in a while." He yawned again, his antennae drooping. "Some of it's just ridiculous, like that post claiming that Exalted Leader was seen with a mysterious Jupiteran woman."

"Yeah, he'd better hope no one mentions that story around Exalted Leader. Because when he's mean, he's *mean*. And when he's nice, he's...he's..."

"Kind of mean," the man finished.

Martian took the watch, reprogrammed it from Plutonian to

GUPPEAS Standard Time, and handed it back to Frink.

"I just read Pietro for the stories about his ex-girlfriend. I saved my favorite one on my communicator." She pulled the communicator out. "He was at some holiday meal with Jam-it and her brother, and the brother brought an automatic gravy-maker built from an old frog-cloner."

He leaned over to read it with her. They were quiet for a few minutes except for occasional giggles. When the Plutonians both doubled over laughing, I knew they'd reached the part where I'd turned the switch and started shooting frogs into the gravy. Even in the freezing cold, my cheeks burned with embarrassment and fury at Pietro.

"Hey," the male Plutonian said, "where's my watch?"

"Maybe you dropped it over there. Or there." They got up to look, moving upriver from us. "You know Pietro must really want that girl back."

"Totally."

When they were out of sight, I got up and stretched. Crouching in the underbrush could be hard on the knees. I opened my mouth to discuss what we should do next.

A hand covered my mouth.

Why was Nlubglub's hand over my mouth?

Nlubglub sprouted another arm and gently turned me around to face two surprised-looking aliens.

They were almost human sized, one aqua and one orange, and each had a pair of tentacles framing a round face. Each alien had four feet: two at the end of their legs, and two attached to stubby append-ages on top of their heads, like antennae designed by a mad cobbler. They wore dusty coveralls, with all four feet bare.

Next to me, Beau turned out his pockets and held up his hands. After a moment, I understood: he was showing that he was unarmed. I followed suit, and the other crew members did the same.

The aliens looked us over with some curiosity (as near as I could tell), moving their tentacles up and down about an inch from our bodies. I wasn't sure if they were looking at us or smelling us. They seemed especially interested in our boots.

The aqua alien curled a tentacle in a gesture whose meaning seemed clear: *Follow me.*

I glanced back to make sure the Plutonians hadn't returned, and then followed the aliens. As we moved away from the ice, the night became balmy, much warmer than Pluto. They led us through the trees until we emerged into a field, with a group of round buildings a few hundred meters away.

"Do you recognize the species?" I whispered to Nlubglub.

"No." Nlubglub peered closely at an alien foot. "And I've studied most of the sentient species in our galaxy."

The aliens led us through a metal gate and into the largest building. The burnt-rubber smell nearly made me gag.

Inside, we found rows of machines, each with a hazardous-looking set of sharp interlocking discs at the top. There were more of the foot-headed aliens, in shades of blue, orange, and brown. Two of them stood on a platform at the top of each machine, pouring in tubs of dirt and rocks, while more aliens operated dials and levers down below. Some of them stopped to gape at us, then scrambled to keep up with the fast-moving machinery.

Frink reached down to pick up a handful of the black-and-white crystals spewing from the bottom end. "Fuelstone."

I took a stone and peered at it. "Fuelstone is Pluto's biggest industry. It's the reason all the other governments make nice with Exalted Leader. And they're taking it from some other planet."

Lola finished the thought for me. "Some planet that they've conquered."

"We don't know that," Beau said. "They could have some sort of secret trade agreement."

"Or the planar dislocator could have just dislocated it by accident," Zeeko said. "I lose stuff like that all the time. My socks keep disappearing out of the laundry room. Maybe they're here somewhere."

"There is no way there should be this many fuelstone processors this close together," Martian said. "One accident and you've got a crater the size of our hometown."

The aqua alien touched a wall panel, and it slid aside to reveal a hidden room big enough for all of us to fit inside without jostling one another. In the corner there was a table stacked with cups, and a device that looked like an industrial-sized water heater.

The smell hit like a shuttlecraft slamming into a dirigible.

"Coffee!" we all gasped simultaneously.

The alien gestured from the cups to the dispenser, and we didn't need a second invitation. We gulped down cup after cup. Even Nlub-glub grabbed a mug, though they couldn't actually drink—they just stood breathing in the essence. My tongue burned, but it didn't matter as I felt long-missing energy coursing through my veins. In that moment, I knew that I loved these aliens and would do whatever it took to protect them.

The orange alien joined us and hit another button, closing the wall panel. They pointed to show us a series of peepholes so we could see what was happening on the factory floor.

"Okay," I said, "what are we supposed to be watching for?"

The two aliens spoke to each other in whistles and chirps that sounded like birdsong.

"Do you understand Jupiteran?" Nlubglub tried the question again with Venusean, Ursan, and a few other languages. When it asked about Plutonian, the aliens responded with more whistles and chirps.

"You understand Plutonian," Beau guessed, "but you can't speak it?"

They nodded, extra feet bobbing.

"You know what we could really use?" I said. "One of those universal translator devices they always have in science fiction movies."

Lola smacked Martian on the arm. "Build us one," she ordered.

"Okay." Martian rubbed his arm. "Do you want that before or after the device to reverse the planar dislocator?"

"After," she said.

"Before," I corrected. "We have to figure out what's going on over here before we go back. Too bad I didn't bring *The Space-Faring*

Moron's Guide to Common Science Fiction Plot Devices."

Frink reached into his tool bag and pulled out a copy of the book.

"Hey, that looks just like the one I had in my…"

Oh.

He followed this with my copy of *Curling Not Hurling,* and a cup holder from Beau's floatcar.

"So, just to review," I said. "We don't know where we are or how to get back. The Plutonians are stealing fuelstone off another planet, and there's nothing we can do about it. We don't have a universal translator, so we're probably going to have to spend the next year learning to speak tentacle-ese. On the plus side, there's coffee."

"And we haven't rescued Pilar Villarreal," Lola added between gulps of coffee. "But they've probably changed our mission by now."

"And what's with the fake Great Frozen River?" Beau asked. "Did the Plutonians want tourists to have somewhere to go when they can't visit the real one? Or maybe they get homesick when they're here stealing fuelstone?"

"Hey." Lola was standing guard at one of the peepholes. "You need to see this."

The rest of us looked through the peepholes. A dozen Plutonians were marching into the factory, including the guards we'd seen earlier. Other than those two, they were in standard Plutonian spacefleet uniforms, except that each had an armband with a conspicuous red button.

"What are those things they're wearing?" I whispered to Martian.

"Not sure," he whispered back. "Maybe a planar recombobulator? I'll tell Frink to snag one for us."

Inside the factory, the Plutonians began shouting in the aliens' birdsong language. Within minutes, they marched back out. The foot-headed aliens followed in a line beside them, walking upside down on their stubby top legs. Their regular legs were being used to push a row of rectangular containers in various colors, each marked with a Plutonian symbol that meant, "Danger! Highly volatile or extremely ticklish contents, or maybe something that just shifts around a lot like beads if you don't pack them right."

Once the Plutonians had left the building, we slipped out and crept along behind them, careful to stay hidden in the foliage. Frink moved ahead of us, right behind the Plutonians, then melted into the underbrush. The Plutonians marched everyone to the spot on the ice where we'd arrived, and the foot-heads stacked up the containers around the target symbol.

The foot-heads backed away, and the Plutonians took their positions around the target. They pushed their armband buttons, and, with a high-pitched whir, they disappeared with the containers in another flash of beige light.

Frink rejoined us. I asked, "Did you get one of those devices?"

"I couldn't. They're attached to the uniforms. I would have had to remove their entire uniform, and that would have attracted attention."

Zeeko grimaced. "And we'd have had to see a Plutonian naked."

For the first and only time, Lola's aura turned pea green.

"Well," Martian said, "at least we know where the target is for the planar recombobulator." He looked expectantly at all of us and got blank looks in return.

Finally, I asked, "What's a planar whatever-it-was?"

"A planar recombobulator is the counterpart to the planar dislocator. When the dislocator sends people to this planet, it can only retrieve them from a specific spot, and only when the recombobulator is activated."

I was more or less following this, which was unusual when Martian talked technology. "So, it's like a beacon?"

"More like a television remote. See, its settings are—"

"Never mind all that," Lola interrupted. "Can you build one?"

"I could, but it would have to be keyed to the original dislocator. Which I can't do without access to the dislocator, which is on Pluto."

"There went Plan A and Plan B," Lola said. "What's C?"

"Plan C is more coffee," Beau said, "so we can focus enough to come up with Plan D." Every time I thought I couldn't like Beau more, somehow he got even better.

We returned to the hidden basement next to the coffee machine and sifted through Plans D through X, and on to Y and Z. Beau poured everyone another round of coffee. Zeeko suggested we use the Betelgeusian alphabet because it had more letters.

Somewhere around Plan Indeterminate Symbol, my beepity-beeper started clanging for the first time since our arrival. I nearly dropped it as I fumbled with the dials, my hands shaking as thoughts of rescue jangled from my head down to my fingertips. "Hello? Hello?"

"Hello," came a vaguely familiar voice. "This is an emergency. I need help!"

"Um, actually—"

"Dr. Villarreal?" Beau said.

"Yes, this is Dr. Pilar Villarreal. I'm being held prisoner on Pluto. There's supposed to be an ambassador from GUPPEAS visiting me, but nobody can find him. Captain Rossi thinks the Plutonians did something to him, and for somebody from a peace organization, she's looking ready to start a war."

My buoyant mood deflated like a defective can of edible air. "Dr. Villarreal? This is Captain Delane. We're trapped on another planet with Ambassador Dangere. How did you get the beepity-beeper to work?"

"I modified the radio in the medical lab. But this is the only channel I've been able to get. What was that about another planet?"

I gave her a quick rundown of what had happened. "We're working on how to get back. I don't suppose your guards left the blueprints for a planar dislocator lying around?"

"No. One of them claims to be trying to design a universal translator, but he can't get it to work."

Martian nearly jumped straight through the beepity-beeper back to Pluto. "Does he have a prototype? Design specs?"

"Just some notes. He wanted me to look at them and compare them with some data on the speech centers of the brain."

Martian's face glowed with excitement. "Can you send the notes to us?"

"I'll upload them. Whoops, have to hurry—looks like that sports thing they're watching is about to end." We heard Plutonians cheering in the background. The notes showed up on the beepity-beeper screen just before the transmission cut off.

Martian read through them with the look of dreamy concentration that meant the pieces were coming together in his head. "I see where they went wrong," he said. "I think I can build one that works. But I'll need some parts. I might have to disassemble the coffee maker."

Lola's aura turned blood red and shot out several inches from her skin. Nlubglub got in between her and Martian, flattening themself into a rubbery purple wall so that her fists bounced off harmlessly. "You are not touching that coffee maker!" she shrieked in a voice that suggested she was plenty caffeinated already.

"Wait," I said. "Why don't you pull some parts from the fuelstone processor? That would keep the Plutonians from stealing any more fuelstone, and it would probably make everyone here a whole lot safer."

We went back out to the factory floor. The sky was growing lighter outside the window, first maroon and then candy-pink. The sleek machines thrummed along, rhythmically pushing out processed fuelstone. "How are you going to disassemble it?" Frink asked.

"That's not a problem," Martian said. "Just have Janet stand next to the machine for a while, and pieces will start falling off."

"That only happened once," I snapped. "And it was totally the mechanic's fault."

A set of interconnected cogs fell off the nearest machine, narrowly missing my head.

I looked at Nlubglub. "Next time Lola wants to kill Martian, don't get in the way."

"Sorry," Nlubglub said, "but I'm the security chief. There are rules about that sort of thing."

"Where's a frog-cloner when you need one?" I muttered, picturing shooting a column of frogs straight at Martian's face.

"I loved that story," Beau said. "That's why *Primarily Pietro* is my favorite blog. Though the one about the keyboard that started writing its own dirty lyrics was pretty good too."

"Pietro exaggerates. I do not have a technology hex, he just—"

A long metal rod fell off the machine, and Beau pulled me out of the way just in time. The rod clanged to the floor. Beau's grip around me loosened, but he didn't let go.

"Thanks," I said.

His face was closer to mine than it needed to be. "Anytime."

8

The Aluminum Brass Knuckles

Martian made a final tweak to the translator, a box about the size of a six-pack of iced coffees. "I think it's done. Give it a try."

I looked nervously at the little aliens. The ones we'd met the first night, aqua and orange, sat slurping coffee in the secret room, watching us with interest.

I cleared my throat. "Hello, I'm Captain Janet Delane, from the Galactic Universal Peacemongering Paradigm Emergent Action Spacefleet." What were the chances of that making sense in another language? It barely made sense in mine.

The blue-green alien chattered back, and the box said tonelessly, "Hello, Captain Janet Delane from the whatever-it-was. What are your pronouns?"

I was a little thrown because the translating voice came from the box. *The Space-Faring Moron's Guide to Common Science Fiction Plot Devices* says that it always comes directly from the alien.

Nlubglub appeared pleased by the civilized question. "The captain's pronouns are 'she' and 'her.' I am Nlubglub, and my pronouns are 'they' and 'them.'" We went around and introduced the crew and Beau.

The orange alien asked, "Are you the Silver Sword?"

"That doesn't make any sense." Martian started to tinker with the machine again. "Maybe it's not working right."

Nlubglub's face flattened into an expression of surprise. "Hang on. The Silver Sword is a figure out of Jupiteran legends. She's supposed to help those who are being oppressed by the Plutonians."

"I am Toecephalus, the District Leader, 'he' and 'him,'" the aqua alien said. Pointing to the orange one, he added, "This is Pinkie, Head of Footwear Acquisitions, 'she' and 'her.'"

"Are you the Silver Sword?" Pinkie asked again.

"No," Nlubglub answered, "none of us is the Silver Sword. The Silver Sword would have to be centuries old. Jupiteran centuries." A Jupiteran century, I recalled vaguely, was somewhere close to 1200 Earth years.

Pinkie's orange foot drooped over her face. "You are not going to free us from the Plutonians? We thought that was why you took the parts off the fuelstone processors. The Plutonians will be angry when they come back and we don't have a full load of fuelstone."

"Of course we'll help you," I said. "I'm...the Aluminum Brass Knuckles."

Martian grinned. "I want to be the Titanium Automatically Reloading Crossbow with Exploding Attachments."

"I'll be the Platinum Tranquilizer Gun," Beau said. "That's peaceful, right?"

By the time Zeeko decided he was the Rubber Spatula, Toecephalus was deep into an explanation of what had happened. "The Plutonians kept appearing and disappearing off that same spot. They seemed friendly enough at first. They learned our language and wanted to trade with us. But when they found out about the fuelstone, everything went crazy."

Beau asked, "Crazy how?"

Pinkie wriggled her tentacles in distress. "We made a deal for the shoes. Amazing shoes. All kinds of them: sling-backs, hiking boots, wedgies, tennis shoes, curling shoes, even those waterproof plastic ones that look horrible but are really, really comfortable. You know the ones?"

"Sure," Beau said. "Everybody has a pair of Gators."

Lola looked scandalized, her aura turning the color of sludge.

Toecephalus continued, "In exchange, we were to mine and

process five hundred tons of fuelstone. It should only have taken five years. But there was a buried clause in the contract that we had to build the replica of the Great Frozen River first. Even after we finished that, the interest rate kept increasing, and every time we thought we were close to having enough fuelstone to pay it off, there was interest on the interest. When we tried to get out of it, they threatened to destroy our coffee crops." His top feet quivered wistfully. "But they were such wonderful shoes."

I looked from him to Pinkie. Both wore pastel jumpsuits and were barefoot. (Bareheaded? Bare-foot-headed?) "So where are these shoes?"

"They're locked into an inaccessible storage tower. We don't get them until the fuelstone delivery is complete." Pinkie rubbed her top feet sadly. "We've been mining for the Plutonians for thirty years now."

"GUPPEAS will want to know about this," Beau said.

I looked out at the darkening magenta sky. "They would, if we knew how to get hold of them."

Beau nodded, stirring his coffee. "Did the Plutonians ever come in a ship?"

"No," Toecephalus said. "They always appear at that spot on the ice."

"Do you have any star charts, so we can figure out where we are?" Frink suggested.

Toecephalus shook his head, toes flopping. "We never mapped the stars. We didn't even know there was life on other planets until the Plutonians showed up."

Nlubglub's smooth purple features were twitching with thought. "How did you know about the Silver Sword?"

Pinkie poured another cup of coffee. "She leaves things for us: secret supplies of weapons and coffee and sports drinks and technology. Plus some cheesy mystery novels for beach reading. Sometimes, she'll leave a supply of shoes hidden for us, but we can't let the Plutonians see them. Until they leave our planet, we all go barefoot." She looked over our uniforms. "Your boots are kind of ugly."

Nlubglub let that pass, probably because they were the only member of the crew not wearing the regulation glow-in-the-dark green boots. "How do you know they're from the Silver Sword?"

"We didn't at first," Toecephalus said, "but some of us have learned to understand the Plutonian language. We can't speak it—our vocal cords aren't twisted enough, I guess—but we hear them talking. They don't know we understand them."

"Is she around now?" I asked. "The Silver Sword?"

"They said a ship was spotted in orbit yesterday, and they thought it was her. But then she got away."

"Maybe she'll be back," I said.

"Maybe." Pinkie gulped her coffee, looking defeated. "How are you going to help us get free of the Plutonians?"

I tried to sound confident. "We're still working on a plan."

The next day we walked over to the storage tower. It was made of unbreakable transparent material, so we could see the giant shoe trees inside, taunting with loafers and cross-trainers and sandals and pointy-toed boots. I think I even saw a pair of clown shoes.

"Still have that lockpick?" I asked Frink. He smiled and pulled the lockpick from his pocket.

"I'm not so sure that's a good idea," Nlubglub said. "But I don't see any cracks I could wiggle through."

"Almost got it," Frink said. He bent his head closer.

A fist-shaped beam of light shot out of the lock and hit Frink in the face, knocking him backward with the lockpick up his nose.

Lola gave the door several powerful kicks. It remained stubbornly sealed. She gave it one more kick for good measure.

"A lock that Frink can't pick," I mused. "And with the planar recombobulator, we've got a technology problem that Martian can't solve. This isn't shaping up well."

"If we find a machine you can't break," Martian said, "we're really in trouble."

"Let's see if I still have my ambassadorial skills," Beau said. "I want to take a look at this contract with the Plutonians."

While Beau worked on that, the crew played a curling match with the foot-heads. Toecephalus and Pinkie used their tentacles for brooms, and they teamed up with Lola and Nlubglub to clobber the rest of us. The outcome included tears, curses, damaged flora, a non-disclosure oath about the score, and Zeeko sweeping in the wrong direction. If they hadn't spotted us a couple of pity points, the game would have qualified for the "Galactic Record Losses" section in *Curling Not Hurling.*

Beau reappeared in the late afternoon. We sat down next to the cacti while he showed us an electronic version of the contract. "It's six hundred pages long. If Martian's translator got it right, there's a nasty little loophole on page 533 that the Plutonians are exploiting. The interest rate can be increased twice a year at Exalted Leader's option. Needless to say, he's been exercising that option every time. If we can get him not to raise the interest at the next delivery date, they'll be able to pay it off."

I scanned through the pages of opaque legalese. "How are we going to persuade him not to do something that obviously benefits him?"

"The usual options would be bribery, blackmail, threats, trickery, and strong-arm tactics. Or using diplomacy and appealing to his better nature."

Lola rubbed her aching foot. "You were kidding on that last one, right?"

"Well, yes. Obviously." Beau gave a rueful smile.

"Right," Lola said. "Now all we have to do is figure out how to get off this planet when we don't even know where we are, convince the Plutonians to stop plundering another planet where they're making a fortune, and not get ourselves killed. While we're at it, why don't we catch that smuggler Nina Mikeljohn and have her cater us a nice dinner, too?"

There was a long silence.

Finally, Zeeko said, "It sounds bad when you put it that way. But on the bright side, there's coffee."

We brainstormed and argued plans until my brain was in knots. After the rest had gone back to the factory, I sat by the edge of the fake Frozen River. The cold air felt surprisingly good as I flipped through the pages of *Curling Not Hurling*. The book claimed that players valued a sporting attitude, and would voluntarily report any accidental violation they committed, such as stepping past the starting line, or using a Saturnian rocklizard in place of a standard stone. The author must never have played against Plutonians.

Something caught my eye downstream, a blur of movement that was dark green but wasn't part of the trees. A Plutonian?

I tried to quietly edge closer. This lasted all of ninety seconds, until I tripped over a lumpy object and fell flat on my face. "Oof!"

The figure morphed into a large green ball that began rolling downhill.

A Jupiteran?

"Wait!" I called, but it sped up instead. The ball became a wheel, rolling faster and faster. By the time I'd pulled myself to my feet, the green wheel had disappeared into the darkness.

None of this made a shred of sense. What was a Jupiteran doing here? Why would it run from me? And what had I tripped over?

The lump turned out to be a duffel bag stuffed with shoes, plus a box of Mars bars and a dozen novels with titles like *Murder on Space Station Z* and *Love's Passionate Cyborg Storm*. There was an off-brand stun gun in the side pocket.

I lugged the bag back to the factory and let myself into the side room. Most of the crew was snoring, but Nlubglub was still awake. I showed them the collection of shoes and described the Jupiteran. "Could that have been the Silver Sword?"

Nlubglub's eyes grew enormous. "You're sure it was a woman?"

"No, I'm not sure of anything. She—or he or they or it—didn't exactly stop to talk. But how many reasons could there be for a

Jupiteran to hang out on a planet occupied by Plutonians?" I poured myself a cup of coffee, my tenth one that day.

Downing ten cups of coffee, just because I could, turned out to be a bad idea. Long after midnight, I was still wide awake, pacing. Finally, I pulled on my glow-in-the-dark boots and went outside.

The night was warm and humid, then quickly turned freezing when I stepped onto the fake Frozen River. I found a flat rock, more or less the right shape for curling. I slid over to the starting line and gave the stone an experimental shove. It veered off to the side and lurched to a stop, nowhere near the target. I retrieved it and tried again. This time, I managed to hit a horned lizard that had been snoozing under the evergreens. The lizard hissed and stalked away into the bushes.

"It's hard to get the spin right." Beau's voice sent a ripple of warmth up and down my freezing spine. He was standing near where I'd found the duffel bag earlier.

"Somehow I don't think I'm going to win the Intra-Galactic Cosmic Curl." I smiled, chafing my arms against the cold.

"You just have to get a feel for it. *Be* the curling stone." He picked up a discarded branch and gave me a mischievous look. "Watch."

He made it look like ballet, dropping to one knee and sliding the stone all in one liquid motion. He stayed down, right arm still extended, his smile lighting up the night under the green glow of three alien moons.

"Gorgeous," he breathed.

"Yes," I said. Then I realized he was talking about the stone, which had come to rest in the exact center of the circle where we'd been dropped on this planet just days before. "I mean, you're right on target."

He pulled himself upright. "Now you try."

I tried to slide gracefully the way he did, but stumbled over a rough spot on the ice. I managed to get the stone moving; then I fell on my face and just missed impaling myself on a spiky plant on the riverbank. Beau pretended not to notice, and swept a path in front of the stone until it stopped in the general vicinity of the target.

For the next one, I stayed upright, but the stone fell far short. "You're not used to the gravity being heavier here than on Pluto," he said. "It would be easier if we had another sweeper."

"No, this is perfect." In a burst of caffeinated energy, I slid the last stone too hard and knocked the other one well past the target. "Or maybe not. Let's trade places."

With some pointers from Beau, I managed to sweep one stone onto the target. "See?" he told me. "We're a good team."

"My fingers are turning blue," I said reluctantly. "Let's get off the ice for a while."

We walked away from the river and onto a pink hillside. Once we got past the freezer units that lined the river, it was a pleasant night. I stretched out on my back and watched the stars, not even minding that I didn't know what to call the constellations or where in the universe we were. "Weird to think that I was supposed to be in a college classroom right about now. Studying, I don't know, Jupiteran literature or space squid psychology. History, maybe. I like history."

"And instead, you're making history by exploring an unknown planet. Not bad for an eighteen-year-old spaceship captain."

It was easier to talk freely when we weren't looking at each other. "Yeah, the reason I like history is that it's mostly about people screwing up. I'm only a spaceship captain because I'm a felon."

"Right. Wanton and mildly atrocious…something. What does that mean, exactly?"

I couldn't believe he remembered that. "There was this meeting where they were going to vote on what to name my town, and I was going to vote for Nerthus—"

"After the earth goddess?"

"You know Nerthus?"

"I'm part Danish. And a little West African, Peruvian, and Thai. And French-Canadian, obviously, or I wouldn't be stuck with a name like Beau Dangere."

"I like your name. It has flair." And I liked the way so many parts of Earth harmonized in such a handsome face. "I'm an excellent judge of names, or I'd have voted to call the town New Industrial Harmony or something."

"Didn't mean to sidetrack you. You were at this meeting…"

I told him the whole story, from the time-traveling shuttle to the painfully brief trial in which I was offered the choice of prison, the military, or GUPPEAS. "No way was I going for the military. My parents are in the military, and I know how much stress it is. They're stationed over by Lyra right now." My voice caught unexpectedly. I'd thought I'd be able to message them for homemade cookies and advice. The constellations looked less friendly now, and everything seemed too far away. "I really miss them."

Beau put a hand on my arm. "Janet, we're going to get off this planet and back to our normal lives. As close to normal as you can be in GUPPEAS, I mean. You'll see your parents again, and you'll get to tell them all about your exploits as a captain, and your first curling victory."

"With mechanical brooms. They'll love the latest about my technology hex." I giggled. "One time when I was twelve, their commanding officer was over at our house, and his sidearm sort of imploded and turned him translucent. He swore I'd done something to it, and honestly, I hadn't even touched it."

"There's probably a perfectly good explanation. What kind of weapon was it?"

"No, it was his actual arm," I admitted. "He was a robot."

"I'm sure it was just a malfunction," Beau said, trying to smother a laugh. "I don't believe this whole Janet the Technology-Slayer story."

"You know my ex calls me Jam-it, right?"

"Sure," Beau said. "I love the frog-cloner story. *Primarily Pietro* is my favorite blog, but that doesn't change the fact that you could do better than him any day. In fact, I know him so well by this point that I'm sure of it."

I said, "He has a big mouth." Which was nowhere near as attractive as Beau's mouth.

"Want to try another end?"

My face warmed. "What?"

"A round of curling," he said. "They call it an end."

"Oh, right. Yes, let's."

We got up and started walking back toward the river. The lizard reappeared, or maybe it was a different one, to hiss at me again. What I had taken for horns were tiny clawed feet on top of its head.

"My turn to ask," I said to Beau. "What crime did you commit to wind up in GUPPEAS?"

"Let's see if you can guess."

"You brought Richena a bouquet of roses, she used them to beat somebody over the head, and you got charged as an accessory."

He smiled. "No, but it did involve Richena. Sort of."

"I knew it! The two of you robbed a coffee shop at laser-point. You stole ten thousand pounds of espresso beans, compressed them into a curling stone, and won the Intra-Galactic Cosmic Curl with it."

He laughed, a deep, warm laugh. "No, but I'll have to try that sometime. There actually was no crime."

"What? That's not possible."

"Not possible that I'm a total choirboy?"

"Not possible that anyone would join GUPPEAS if they didn't have to."

He shrugged. "I was interested in a diplomatic career, and there weren't a lot of openings for someone under a hundred years old. And Richena had just joined, and I decided to go with her."

"And Richena's crime was...?"

He moved ahead so I couldn't see his face. "You'd have to ask her about that."

"Says the diplomat." We reached the river and started gathering the stones back up. "Did you always know you wanted to be an ambassador?"

"Pretty much." He found the discarded brooms. "I seem to thrive on drama. Probably comes from having eight sisters and brothers. You sort of remind me of my sister Bonbon."

"Is that short for Bonita?" I slid a stone, but he didn't go after it to sweep.

"No, it's just Bonbon. They ran out of names. She was the one who'd be designing environmentally sustainable jet packs for dogs or something, while everyone else would get into some silly argument over breakfast and start throwing croissants. I negotiated my first peace treaty among my siblings."

"Well, that explains what you're doing engaged to Richena." I was getting onto thin ice here, and not just on the river.

"We are not engaged," he said quickly. "We broke up months ago. And I mean really broke up, not that on-and-off thing we used to do. Problem is, the Plutonians have very strong beliefs about soulmates, and they wouldn't think much of an ambassador who couldn't keep his own relationship together. I shouldn't have let Richena talk me into faking a relationship, but if I tell the Plutonians now, it'll just make things worse."

"And she told Pietro you were engaged, and got him to put it in the *Galactic Times*. Pretty sneaky." I slid another stone. "What did you even see in her?"

He didn't seem offended. "What can I say? I like bad girls."

"And now you're working for an organization full of felons. Those seem like good odds."

"There's definitely no shortage of drama in GUPPEAS. I fit right in." He came up behind me, gently correcting my grip on the broom.

My heart was pounding like a washing machine with a broken belt. I kept my voice steady, trying not to notice how warm his skin felt against mine. "No wonder we get along so well. Chaos seems to follow wherever I go."

"Somehow, felon or not, you are an incurably good girl."

I turned to face him. "I'm curling in the middle of the night with someone else's fake fiancé. How good could I be?"

He bent closer, and his mouth was moving toward mine like a shuttle to the docking bay.

The beige light erupted over the ice target, and we had just enough time to throw ourselves behind the underbrush before the planar dislocator dropped in the newest arrival.

I expected a company of soldiers like before, but instead there was just one Plutonian in a long dark cloak. We caught a brief glance at his face as he looked around furtively; then he headed in the direction opposite the foot-head settlement.

I looked at Beau and whispered, "Was that…?"

"Exalted Leader," Beau whispered back, "looking awfully guilty about something."

Exalted Leader moved slowly, unused to the heavier gravity. We followed him at a safe distance. There were no more duffel bags or other obstacles to trip over. After half an hour, we reached a house with jagged red stalactites accenting the roof in the traditional Plutonian style. He punched a code into the keypad on the door, and it opened. Before Beau and I could move closer, it slid shut behind him.

"Vacation home?" I wondered aloud. "War room for imperialist plots?"

"Secret bunker in case of overthrow on Pluto?" Beau suggested.

"Or maybe he has a girlfriend."

Beau raised an eyebrow. "Whatever it is, we'd better find out. This might be our ticket home."

9

Like a Curling Stone

We went back to the factory, and eventually I fell asleep in the hidden room, despite Lola snoring, Martian muttering formulas in his sleep, and Zeeko sleep-waltzing.

In the morning, several items were missing from the duffel bag. I shook Frink awake. "You have one minute to give back the shoes and the stun gun, or I'm going to force you to read that entire Plutonian contract, all 600 pages."

Frink yawned and ran a hand through his leafy green hair. "I hollowed out a space in the wall behind the coffee machine."

I found the spot and pulled out the missing shoes as well as some Plutonian currency and Richena Rossi's appointment book. "Martian, see if you can fix this." I slid the datebook into his hand, hiding the cover from Beau. "We'll give the shoes to Toecephalus to remove the temptation. Frink, where's the stun gun?"

His orange eyes were starting to focus. "There was a stun gun?"

"Frink, do we really have to go through this every time you steal something?"

"No, Captain. That would take too long. But I didn't see a stun gun. Maybe Martian took it for parts?"

"No," Martian said, pocketing the appointment book and heading for the coffee machine. "But I could find a use for it. I have this neat idea for an extreme flashlight. What kind of stun gun was it?"

"The kind that isn't here." Lola first thing in the morning was even more irritable than normal Lola. "Speaking of which, Captain, I noticed you and Ambassador Dangere weren't here last night. Anything we should know?"

I turned a bright pink that could probably match Lola's aura.

Beau was unflappable. "Yes, Exalted Leader paid a little visit."

Beau and I described the Plutonian leader's arrival and his visit to the house with the stalactites. We left out a few details, like my disastrous curling performance and the almost-kiss.

Nlubglub bounced nearly to the ceiling with excitement. "Exalted Leader has to be the one to raise the interest rate for the fuelstone, right? So what if there were no Exalted Leader?"

"We don't do assassinations," I said. "We're a peace organization."

"Right. But what if he's forced to resign or gets fired or however you get rid of an Exalted Leader?" Nlubglub's entire face morphed into a Cheshire Cat–like grin. "If there's no one in office when the deadline passes, they can't do anything about it."

"That might work," I said, "but I don't see how—"

"If I could meditate, I'd come up with something, but I can't concentrate without my meditation crystal." Lola glared at Frink. "Why didn't you steal it and bring it with us?"

"What about kidnapping Exalted Leader?" Frink suggested quickly. He looked a little too happy about the idea. "We wouldn't have to hurt him. Kidnapping's the same as stealing, except it's a person, right?"

All eyes turned to me.

"I don't think GUPPEAS Command would go for that," I said. After a moment, I added, "But they're not here, and we don't have any way to contact them to ask for orders."

Later, while the rest of the crew went out exploring, I stayed in the secret room with Martian and helped him examine Richena's electronic appointment book. "I don't see anything wrong with it," he said, peering at the circuits.

"That can't be right. She had a hair appointment on Pluto at the same time as a power lunch on Earth."

He reached for a smaller screwdriver. "Maybe she wrote it down wrong. Or maybe she's as bad with technology as you are."

"Watch it!" I elbowed him. "If you weren't my brother—"

"—then I'd be home in New Harmony Whatever instead of here in some other galaxy, dodging Plutonians."

"And you'd have never seen a planar dislocator or invented the universal translator," I said.

"Good point." He touched a wire on the datebook, and a tiny hologram appeared of Richena and Beau holding hands. I grimaced. Martian gave me a half-smile, then separated the wires and the hologram dissipated. "Why the interest in Richena Rossi?"

"I think she's up to something with that sealed-off storage bay."

"Really? It isn't about her relationship with Beau Dangere?"

I made a show of looking closely at the circuits. "I have no idea what you're talking about."

"Janet. When I talk propulsion systems and irradiated particles, you have no idea what I'm talking about. But it's hard to miss that look Beau keeps giving you."

"That's totally not—Wait, what kind of look?"

"Sort of like the interior of a solar-powered musical diamond drill," he said.

"What?"

Martian just grinned and switched tools again.

"I hate you," I said. "Anyway, what do you know about relationships? Look at what happened with you and that Lyran exchange student."

"What did happen? I went to put together the universal remote for all the gadgets in the house, and the next thing I knew she was gone."

I sighed. "You spent six weeks on that thing, trying to make the microwave remote-cook food that was still in the fridge. I don't think you looked up once during that time. Maybe you should only date other engineers. Or robots."

"Oh, Janet. Nobody dates robots anymore." He selected some pieces from among the disassembled parts. "I'm going to put these in the sanitizer gun I've been working on."

"What for?"

"Come on, how long have we been on this planet?" he said. "Our uniforms all stink, and so do we. Except Lola—for some reason, she always smells like paprika."

I watched him work in silence for a while, his round face fixed in concentration. Finally, I asked, "Do you think it's true that guys like bad girls?"

"Like, bad how? Are we still talking about Lola?" he said. "She seems like someone who'd have an ex or two buried underneath her quarters."

"She's doing much better with her anger issues, now that she has the meditation crystal. Or so she tells me." I had my doubts. "But what I meant was, hypothetically, if a man said he liked drama and bad girls, do you think I'd have a chance?"

"Sure."

"Really?"

"Sure, as long as you had a total personality transplant, incinerated the GUPPEAS rule book, and got arrested for something better than a floatcar accident. At least jaywalk between two adjacent moons or something." Martian's eyes glowed the clear blue of a computer screen. "On this planet, they'd call you a goody-four-shoes. You'll be a bad girl the day that I become a Luddite, Lola becomes a Zen master, Frink gives up stealing, Nlubglub marries a Plutonian, and Zeeko says something that makes sense."

I managed not to throw any tools at him. "Did you have to say that about Nlubglub marrying a Plutonian? That image is going to give me nightmares."

"That part? Not the part about you jaywalking? Maybe there's hope."

"I've been wondering about something." A half-formed theory was taking shape in my mind. "No one seems to know how Zeeko wound up on the ship, and when I asked that GUPPEAS bureaucrat about it, he'd never heard of anyone by that name. And is it really possible for anyone to be as clueless as Zeeko seems to be?"

"It's not exactly a lack of cluefulness." Martian finished putting the datebook pieces into the sanitizer gun. "It's more like you're doing a crossword, and he's giving you instructions for cooking risotto, in a random order, possibly in some language with no alphabet. It makes sense to him, just not to anyone else."

"But he was the one who hit the button on the planar dislocator. And now the stun gun's missing and Frink swears he doesn't have it, which I admit is hard to believe. So I started wondering: what if there isn't a Plutonian saboteur? What if Zeeko's the saboteur, and this is all an elaborate ruse? Is that even remotely possible?"

A moment passed. Then we said it together:

"No."

Martian pointed the sanitizer gun at me. "Hold still." I was enveloped in a pale mist. The pink grass stains disappeared from my uniform, and I smelled like a new floatcar.

A moment later, the door opened and Beau came in, followed by the rest of the crew. "We saw the fuelstone mine," Beau told us. "They've trained large insects to burrow into the ground so they can reach the fuelstone."

"I never thought about training insects," Zeeko said. "I used to train lizards to act out famous movie scenes."

"They were pretty good," Nlubglub added.

Lola made a so-so gesture. "Not so much with the drama scenes, but the dance numbers weren't bad. Their claws worked as tap shoes."

I had never heard this. "So why did you stop?"

"Frink kept stealing them," Zeeko said, "and then they'd escape and eat all the fuelstone and start little fires every time they got the hiccups. We finally let them loose in a swamp on Titan, and they did the finale from *A Chorus Line* to say goodbye."

I went to pour myself some coffee. "You smell nice," Beau said, appearing next to me. "Want to get in some more curling practice?"

"Later. Martian and I need to finish something."

A dispute broke out between Lola, Nlubglub, and Frink over whose turn it was to wash coffee cups. I watched as Beau went to practice diplomacy.

Martian said, "I think he likes good girls better than he thinks he does."

"Really?" I asked. "How much does he like them?"

Martian gave me a shrewd look. "As much as I'd like to check out that planar recombobulator with a reticulated sonic laser inspector."

"I think I understood that one."

Three days later, my crew was in the middle of another disastrous curling match with Toecephalus and Pinkie when the beige light flashed on the target again. By now, it was almost a reflex for us to hide behind the trees. Exalted Leader appeared with a unit of Plutonian guards. He was wearing even more medals than the day we'd met him, including one shaped like a coffee pot with a slash through it.

Once again, the Plutonians forced the foot-heads to pack the fuelstone into storage containers, which were color-coded according to some system I couldn't understand. We watched from behind the trees as the foot-heads pushed a line of coffin-sized containers up the river, with the guards looming over them. When half of the fuelstone containers were arranged around the target, a Plutonian guard hit the button on his armband. There was a shrill whistling sound that made Zeeko cover his oversized ears in pain, and the containers disappeared.

The foot-heads began pushing the final load up the ice. "We need to get in with the containers somehow," Lola whispered.

I turned and nearly jumped. A purple fuelstone container was sitting where Nlubglub had been a moment before. It sprouted a mouth and spoke in Nlubglub's voice. "This would work, but it's not big enough to hold everyone."

"You don't have to hold everyone," I said. "Just Martian. Then he can figure out how to operate the planar dislocator, and we'll steal another of those beacons, and he can bring us back when the Plutonians aren't around."

"That's the plan?" Lola asked. "Seriously?"

Martian climbed inside the faux fuelstone container. "There's room for one more." Nlubglub's voice was muffled with Martian inside.

I had to make a fast decision. Lola was second-in-command, so it would make sense to put her in charge of the crew on Pluto—besides which, she'd find some way to punish me if I didn't send her back. But Frink would be the most help to Martian in figuring out the planar dislocator. Zeeko would most likely be a hindrance to whomever had him.

"Take Ambassador Dangere," I said. "He needs to get back before Richena causes an interplanetary incident."

"Are you sure?" Beau asked.

Was I sure that I wanted the most attractive man I'd ever met to go back to Pluto where Richena was waiting, and leave me stranded here? "No time to argue! Go!" The Plutonians were going to be gone soon. Beau's hand brushed against mine as I helped him squeeze into the cramped space with Martian. Nlubglub closed their lid.

Seeing what was happening, Toecephalus and Pinkie ran in front of the nearby guards and started a loud argument to distract them. The rest of us heaved Nlubglub and their hidden passengers out onto the ice. They landed directly in front of a Plutonian, who started berating the foot-heads about having missed one.

They moved Nlubglub onto the target with the other containers, and then Exalted Leader said something to his second-in-command. The loud whining noise came again, and the containers disappeared along with all of the Plutonians—except for Exalted Leader.

Toecephalus and Pinkie went back inside the factory with the rest of the foot-heads. Exalted Leader set off in the other direction.

"Should we follow him?" Lola whispered.

"I know where he's going," I said.

He was headed toward the Plutonian house.

We watched the house from a distance as the downstairs lights went dark and an upstairs one came on. Lola turned to me. "Should we try to sneak in, or snag him when he comes out?"

"You really think we should kidnap him?" At this point, I wasn't sure if I wanted to be talked into it or out of it. "That's not exactly a misdemeanor."

"Whatever they do to us, it can't be worse than being stuck on this planet," Lola said. "Let's find a way in there and grab Exalted Leader. Anyone got a problem with that?"

I was pretty sure I'd regret this. "Let's do it."

"Who does the actual grabbing?" That was Zeeko. "There's too many of us to all do it."

"Whoever's closest to him," I said. "And Frink, no taking his wallet."

"Um, okay," he said in an agreeable tone that told me his klepto-maniac brain was looking for loopholes.

"Or jewelry or any other valuables," I added. "Or non-valuables. Not even socks. Now, how are we going to get in?"

"The shoe tower busted my electronic lockpick, and my regular ones are back in the factory basement. We could break down the door, I guess."

"Um, guys?" Lola stage-whispered from above us. "Up here."

Lola was sitting on the windowsill just above our heads. She gave us a wave and climbed the rest of the way inside. Frink followed with the ease of an experienced burglar. He pulled Zeeko up after him, and I heard a thump. "Everything okay?" I called.

"Just landed on my head," Zeeko answered. "At least, I think I did. It's hard to tell in this room." Frink reached a hand down for me.

I was too short to reach him. He leaned down as far as he could without falling, and I tried to jump. Our fingertips almost touched.

"Come on, already!" Lola hissed.

I looked around and saw a green storage container at the corner of the house. Good enough. I dragged it over, climbed on top, and pulled myself in through the window.

We appeared to be in the living room, if "living" was the right word for a freezing cold room with a lumpy crater in the middle, in dark purple and orange. The ceiling had a crater too, or that may have been an illusion created by the rows of mirrors along the walls. The sagging couch was covered in fuzzy cushions, and two matching chairs bookended an elaborate carved table. The place gave off the moldy smell of Pluto. In between the mirrors hung posters of Jupiter-an films.

"Queelchu," Zeeko whispered.

"Gesundheit," I answered automatically.

"No, Queelchu. The famous Jupiteran actress."

"Oh, right," Frink said. "From when they still made movies in only three dimensions." The posters all showed the same green Jupiteran woman, morphed into a variety of shapes: aiming four guns at once in the poster for *Invasion of the Psychic Laser Vampires*, striking a sexy pose for *Astro-Babes*. "Wonder if any of these posters are valuable?"

"Not now!" I whispered. I could hear footsteps coming down the hall. "Be quiet!" We dove behind the furniture.

Exalted Leader walked into the room.

He took one look at the mirrors and saw us.

He ran for the door.

A dark yellow ray flashed from Lola's hand to Exalted Leader's head. He twitched, wobbled, and fainted into the crater in the floor.

I stared at Lola. "You took the stun gun?"

Zeeko tackled me.

"Zeeko," I said. "We're not kidnapping me. We're kidnapping Exalted Leader."

His forehead scrunched in confusion. "But you said whoever's closest."

"Never mind," I said. "Is he all right?"

Frink checked Exalted Leader's pulse. "He's fine." He took out a penknife and cut off Exalted Leader's uniform sleeve, the part with the large red button. "I think this is one of those planar things we can use to signal Martian to bring us back."

I got up and dusted myself off. "Lola, I'm not sure you're clear on the concept of this peace organization thing."

"So write me up when we get home. Let's get him out of here."

Dull green flesh flopped and jiggled as we dragged him down the stairs and out of the house.

I peered around the corner to see if the coast was clear. Four uniformed Plutonians were marching toward the house, which probably qualified as the coast being not clear. "We have to hide him."

I stepped backward and nearly tripped over another green storage container. "Was this here before?"

"It's here now," Lola said, and stuffed Exalted Leader inside it.

We started pushing the container back toward the river. "Try to look nonchalant," I said.

"I don't know, I'm feeling pretty chalant," Zeeko said.

A whispering sound was coming from inside the storage container, but I wasn't going to open it up to ask what he'd said.

The Plutonians were close now, all armed with wicked-looking lasers. Standard-issue Plutonian military lasers had a dozen settings from "lightly kill" to "annihilate." These lasers looked bigger than the standard-issue ones.

Our paths crossed right at the frozen river's edge.

"Halt," the commander said. "Who are you? What are you doing?"

I could have really used Beau right about then to charm the guys with the big guns. I tried to improvise. "We're from GUPPEAS. We've been asked to dispose of this load of highly contaminated fuelstone waste."

The container jolted forward. Zeeko and Frink held it down with all their might.

"You can see how unstable it is," Frink added. "It's so dangerous, we can't even keep it on the planet."

The Plutonians took a step back. "Where are you taking it?"

I could see the ice target from here, the same one we'd been using in curling practice. "Jupiter. We're taking it to Jupiter. They have, uh, facilities to deal with this sort of thing." The target was tauntingly close. "We just need to get it to the pickup spot down there."

"On whose orders?" the commander persisted.

"Exalted Leader's, of course."

The container rocked back and forth. "Extremely volatile," Lola added. "We'd better get going."

We started to walk away. All we had to do was get to the target, Frink would activate the planar recombobulator, and if Martian was doing his job, we'd disappear from here. Not far now. If we could just keep them convinced.

A shrill voice sounded from right under our feet. "He's inside! Exalted Leader's inside! Help!"

No time to think. The Plutonians reached for their weapons, but I was faster. I shoved the container into them, knocking three of them down. The fourth one snarled and shoved it back at me. I jumped out of the way, and the container slid on the ice. And kept sliding.

A voice from the container screamed again for help. The Plutonian ran after it, and the other three were scrambling to their feet.

I ran past them, threw myself on top of the container, and held on tight.

The container whirled around for an exhilarating minute, trees and spiky bushes whooshing past. On the first spin, I saw Lola take down a Plutonian with her stun gun. On the second spin, the last one up from the ground made a grab for the gun. Lola used her free hand to punch him in the face, knocking him into a bush. He squealed in pain.

I was headed toward a nasty-looking spiky plant. Getting impaled would be an undignified end to the mission. Beau's voice echoed in my head: *Be the curling stone.* I shifted my weight, aiming toward the target, and missed the plant by an inch.

The container's curl across the ice was slowing down, and the target was still out of reach. I wasn't going to make it, not if I wanted to hang on to Exalted Leader.

"Brooms!" I hollered at Frink and Zeeko.

Zeeko pulled a branch off the nearest tree and ran over to where I was sliding. Frink grabbed another branch and ran to join him. Shouting directions back and forth, they swept the ice, clearing a path toward our escape. As the container spun around, I saw the third Plutonian was flat on his face. The fourth had dropped her weapon and was running away at top speed. Lola took aim.

I sailed to a perfectly targeted stop on the target. Frink, Zeeko, and then Lola crowded around.

"Oh wow!" Zeeko gasped. "I swept in the right direction!"

Frink threw down his broom. "We are totally gonna crush Pluto in the Intra-Galactic Cosmic Curl!"

Then everything around us faded to black.

10

A Planet Not Called Janet

I got hit with that feeling of being stretched out and squashed back together, and then the light came on. We'd returned to the factory on Pluto, next to the planar dislocator. Martian, Nlubglub, and Beau were sitting at the controls.

Martian grabbed me in a hug. "We did it!"

"And look what we brought with us." Lola threw open the storage container. Exalted Leader stared up at us miserably.

Martian released me, and I turned to Beau, who reached out for a handshake. "Congratulations, Captain." It took a moment to realize why he was being so distant: we were back on Pluto, back to our regular lives, and he was still Richena's fake fiancé. But his hand didn't seem to want to let go. Not when I'd just done something indisputably, irresistibly bad.

Zeeko tried to help Exalted Leader up, but he ignored the offered hand and pulled himself out of the container. "Byufulus Fedderbang put you up to this, didn't he? Whatever he's paying you, I can double it."

"He's paying us four hundred million credits," Frink said quickly. "Apiece."

"We're not taking a bribe," I said. "And we're not working for whoever that was. We're here to free the people that you have enslaved at your fuelstone plants."

"They're not enslaved," he said, slipping back into his usual arrogant tone. "They signed a legally binding—"

"Save it," Beau interrupted. "The only thing we want to hear from you is that they've fulfilled their contract, they get their shoes, and they owe you nothing. And you're going to announce it at the public meeting today that we've already arranged, with cameras beaming it all over your planet. Otherwise, there's going to be a massive fuelstone boycott that will destroy Pluto's economy."

A small, squeaky voice came from behind us. "I don't think so."

Lola reached for the stun gun, but it was no longer in her pocket. Instead, it was held by a Jupiteran woman in a familiar shade of green.

I groaned. "You were the storage container. I can't believe I didn't see that coming."

"Especially since we used the same trick," Zeeko added helpfully.

"Hey," Nlubglub said, "you're Queelchu! I love your movies, especially the one about the radioactive penguin that falls in love with the—"

"Shut up!" the actress said. "Nobody on Jupiter has cared about my movies in decades. I'd like to blow up the whole planet, paint all the pieces ugly colors, and shoot them into the sun! They don't appreciate me. No one does, except for Fibby." She gave Exalted Leader an adoring look.

"Fibby?" Beau said. "Fibbreous Nekwizzle, the Exalted Leader of Pluto, is *Fibby*?"

"He's my leading man." By now I recognized her voice as the one that had been calling for help from the storage container.

"And she's the love of my life," Exalted Leader simpered. "As green as the skies over Pluto, or that fuzzy moss that grows on the palace walls."

"But—but—but you're Jupiteran!" Nlubglub sputtered. "He's Plutonian! Our planets have been at war seventy-six times just in my lifetime. You two together, that's—that's—I don't even have a word for what that is, and I speak thirty-one languages. It just doesn't happen."

Queelchu coolly looked Nlubglub over. "Says who?"

Nlubglub looked ready to dissolve from sheer horror. "Our planets are at war right this minute."

"He started that war for me." Her eyes shone with an ardor that would have been touching if she hadn't been pointing a weapon at us.

"They deserved it," Exalted Leader said. "She should have won a Golden Galaxy Award for her last movie, and they didn't even nominate her." He caressed her rubbery green face.

"Wow," Beau said. "And I thought I'd had some screwed-up relationships."

Queelchu jerked the stun gun toward the door. "Move," she said. "We're going to this meeting, and Fibby can announce an increase in fuelstone production. And those shoe nuts can just keep paying up."

Seven of us, two of them. One stun gun. Those didn't seem like impossible odds. I moved to the side, out of her direct line of sight. I caught Beau's eye, then looked pointedly at the stun gun.

Beau gave the slightest nod and a twitch of a smile to let me know he understood. He stepped directly in front of Queelchu, keeping her attention. "Is Fibby also going to announce your impending marriage?" He arched an eyebrow. "Oh no, of course not—you have to keep this little romance a secret, don't you?"

"Shut up!" Queelchu said, but I got the feeling they'd had this argument before, and he'd touched a nerve. If Jupiterans had nerves.

"People wouldn't understand," Exalted Leader said.

Lola's aura turned a deep puce. "Sacrificing your career and hiding out on some remote planet, just so he can stay in office? What woman would do that anymore?"

"None that I know," Beau said.

"Our captain wouldn't," Zeeko said, "and she doesn't even like her career."

That may or may not be the reason Queelchu sprouted an eye to look at me, the same moment I dove for the stun gun.

For the second time that day, everything went dark.

I regained consciousness in Exalted Leader's floatcar, nauseous and sore. Why did my head feel like somebody had been practicing curling shots inside it?

Beside me, Beau groaned as he dragged his eyes open.

Oh, right. The stun gun. Queelchu was still pointing it at my crew while Exalted Leader drove.

We docked outside the Plutonian capitol building, and Exalted Leader opened the hatch. A half-dozen armed guards were waiting outside. Where Queelchu had stood a moment before, there was a podium in the now-familiar shade of dark green. "Lift the podium gently," Exalted Leader ordered us, "and carry it to the common room." The guards followed.

The common room was crowded with Plutonians, and a handful of reporters from off-world. Exalted Leader handed the stun gun to one of the guards and had us set the green podium on a dais in the center of the cavernous room.

"Fellow citizens of Pluto!" he began. "I come to announce wonderful news." He glanced down at Queelchu, and for a moment he got misty-eyed. I could sense how much he loved her, how much he wanted to break down and confess the truth about his love affair.

But he squared his floppy shoulders, smiled directly into the camera, and said, "Our production of fuelstone…"

He stopped.

His face traveled a slow arc from smugness to confusion, to fear, to quivering panic. His jowls shook and his eyes bulged horribly at something behind me.

I turned.

Foot-heads were pouring in by the dozens. No, not dozens—hundreds. Maybe more. They kept coming, clutching every weapon imaginable: clubs, lasers, nunchucks, even a titanium automatically reloading crossbow with exploding attachments. At the front of the army stood Toecephalus, wielding a silver sword.

They were all wearing shoes.

Each of them had two pairs, the ones on their heads mismatched with the ones underneath. Steel-toed boots. Running shoes. Strappy sandals. Those waterproof plastic shoes that look ridiculous but are really, really comfortable. Some of the crowd wobbled a bit in high heels, and one stopped to switch her stilettos with the flats on her top feet. Still, they kept coming.

The guards dropped their weapons and ran for the rear exit. The other Plutonians followed, trying to climb over each other in a panic. But now more foot-heads were coming in the back door. There was nothing for us to do but stand back in wonder, watching.

The podium resumed her normal shape as Queelchu, and she threw herself in front of Exalted Leader, trying to shield him. "Don't hurt my Fibby!"

The first row of foot-heads charged into them at full speed, head-first like bulls. Exalted Leader and Queelchu both went flying, landing in the balcony seats. Another Plutonian jumped up and shrieked, "That's a Jupiteran!"

Newly shod feet kicked Plutonian butts all over the place. Plutonians zoomed through the air from the impact. The ones hit by stiletto heels simply keeled over, squealing in pain. One fast runner almost got around us; he was downed by a thrown boot.

Within minutes, the room was littered with shoes and moaning Plutonians. Toecephalus flung himself down next to me, lying on his back with all four feet wiggling at the ceiling, chattering away in his own language.

Pinkie came trotting over with the universal translator balanced on her top feet. "That was fun!" She held a pair of aluminum brass knuckles.

I looked around at the mayhem. "How did you get here?"

Toecephalus sat up, brimming with excitement. "The Silver Sword left the door to the tower open. Not only was it full of shoes, but she left us piles of weapons. There was a note telling us to go to the target spot on the ice, and she transported us to the factory. There was a ship outside to bring us here."

"The Silver Sword?" I tried to take this in. "Did you see her?"

"No," Pinkie said. "But we know it was her."

"She left us this, stuck in the door of the shoe tower." Toecephalus raised his silver sword in a salute. The other foot-heads gave a mighty cheer.

"That's it!" shouted one of the Plutonians, pulling herself to her feet. She had a crossbow bolt sticking out of an antenna, but she didn't seem to notice. "Just you wait! You think you had it bad before? There's a whole planet full of us Plutonians, and you just got yourself a war!"

The other Plutonians called out in agreement, though not too loudly, since they were still in pain. The foot-heads reached for their weapons. Things were going to get ugly if someone didn't act fast.

What would a real captain do?

I ran to the dais where Exalted Leader had been a few minutes earlier. Grabbing the microphone, I yelled, "Hold it!"

Eyes and eyestalks all over the room turned in my direction.

I had no idea what to say.

I steadied my hands around the microphone and forced myself to speak up. "You don't want a war."

"Sure we do," the Plutonian woman explained pleasantly as she finally pulled the crossbow bolt out of her antenna. "Weren't you listening?"

Lola moved closer, her fist tightening. I gave a warning look, and Lola backed off.

"What has war ever gotten you?" I asked. "You lose lives, waste money, and wind up with a leader who bans chocolate and coffee. Is that really what you want?"

There were a few murmurs and nods. The reporters moved around the room, filming everything. Pietro was in the back, typing notes into his communicator. His aura shone a bright royal purple that I hadn't seen since our first date.

I pushed on. "You could have made a deal for the fuelstone. You could have sold the technology for the planar dislocator." I saw Martian's face light up at the mention. "Instead, you got yourselves totally humiliated, and it's being broadcast in the news on every planet that's ever heard of you. You can do better than this. You can have peace, prosperity, and billiard matches without any rioting."

"The billiard riot was Jupiter's fault!" somebody yelled.

"Was not!" Nlubglub yelled back, looking around for the offender.

"Stop it!" The microphone nearly slipped out of my sweaty hands. Squashing down my nervousness, I used my most authoritative voice. "If you start another war, sooner or later you'll go through a disaster like this all over again, and you won't be able to blame anyone but yourselves."

"Sure we can," said another Plutonian. "We can blame Exalted Leader. Look at him over there with his Jupiteran girlfriend. It's all their fault!"

"Yes, look at them." Beau took the microphone from me. "They've found the love of their lives. How many people are ever that lucky? How many of us are struggling along from one drama-filled relationship to the next, always looking for that one person who's a perfect fit? They found their soulmate. They found love."

"But she's a Jupiteran!" someone else yelled.

"Yes," Beau answered. "And they were able to look past their differences and find what really mattered. If you learn to look past your differences, you could live in peace with your neighbors. And maybe even something better."

Someone in the back started to applaud. I caught a glimpse of a mass of curly blonde hair and recognized Nina the smuggler. How had she gotten in here? My crew joined the applause, and the foot-heads started clapping their top feet. Then Exalted Leader and Queelchu joined in, and a few of the Plutonians, and then more, and finally the whole room was giving us a standing ovation.

Beau looked at me, and my heart started to pound. He gave a smile that could outshine a supernova.

Things moved fast from there. The next day, Beau accompanied my crew to a meeting with a Plutonian I recognized: the mayor who'd presided over our curling match. He was decked out with a few new medals, including one with tiny print that roughly translated as, "Didn't screw up too much."

"Captain Janet Delane, you remember Byufulus Fedderbang,"

Beau told me. "He's in charge now that Fibbreous Nekwizzle has resigned."

"Nekwizzle was a total failure," Fedderbang said. "He actually seemed relieved to be stepping down. He and Queelchu are going to start an inter-species dating service."

"So you're the new Exalted Leader?" I asked.

"The title of Exalted Leader can lead to delusions of grandeur," he said, wiping away a spot of mold on the desk. "Henceforth, I shall be known as Adequate Leader."

"That's great, um, Your Adequacy," I said. "Adequate leadership is exactly what this planet needs."

"The council is making some changes," Adequate Leader went on. "We're meeting with representatives from Jupiter to put an end to hostilities."

Nlubglub looked impressed. Lola's aura turned a bright shade of gold.

My beepity-beeper rang, and I discreetly glanced at it. Message from Pietro? No time to worry about that right now.

"Also," Beau said, "the caffeine ban has been lifted, and Dr. Villar-real will go home with you."

Cheers erupted from the crew. Zeeko yelled, "Let's go find some coffee!" He, Frink, and Lola raced from the room. I grabbed Martian with one hand and Nlubglub with the other, trying to maintain some shred of decorum.

Toeccphalus and Pinkie were escorted in by a Plutonian honor guard, and Pinkie deposited the universal translator on the table. Toecephalus was wearing cowboy boots on his lower feet and shiny tap shoes on his head; Pinkie had opted for pink ballet slippers and curling shoes. Several other foot-heads crowded in behind them, all elegantly shod.

"Welcome," Adequate Leader said to them. "We'll make the planar dislocator available to get your people home. Feel free to go shoe-shopping first, if you'd like. After we pay your back wages, of course."

"That would be very nice," Pinkie said.

"Also," Beau said, "GUPPEAS would like to work out an agreement for more fuelstone, but at a fair price and prepaid. Let me repeat: prepaid."

"We'll want our lawyers to look over the documents this time," Toecephalus answered, "but I think we can work something out."

Beau nodded. "I'll start drawing up an agreement between GUPPEAS and…I'm sorry, I don't know what to call you. What's the name of your planet?"

"We just call it Planet," Pinkie said. "But now that we're in contact with other worlds, we have a committee trying to decide on a name."

"How long have they been working on it?"

"Thirty years," she admitted. "Ever since we met the Plutonians."

I tried not to groan. "You're going to fit right in with GUPPEAS. Look, forget the committee. Just pick a good name." I was thinking along the lines of Planet Janet—it was kind of fun to say.

"I've got it!" my brother said. "You can be Martians!"

"That won't work," I said. "There's already a Mars."

"So we'll call the planet Martia."

"That's a great name," Toecephalus said. "And it's fun to say. Martia!"

"Martia, Martia, Martia!" the newly dubbed Martians chanted.

I felt like I'd just been smacked in the nose.

My brother looked at me. "Something wrong, Jan?"

"Not a thing." I walked away, muttering, "Martia, Martia, Martia," under my breath.

Back in my quarters, I sent a note to my parents, letting them know my first official mission was a success. I scanned the news: a goodwill game of curling set up for Jupiter and Pluto, the return of chocolate and coffee, and a successful mission by someone else contacting the giant space squid. I kept scrolling until I ran across a picture of Beau with his "fiancée."

I switched off the news and answered Pietro's message. Five

minutes later, I'd agreed to meet him for coffee.

The coffee place had been redecorated in a cheerful shade of red and smelled heavenly. "They've already got seventeen different kinds of coffee," Pietro marveled. We snagged the last empty table and settled in with our drinks: ionized coffee-nitrogen shot for him, mocha with whipped cream for me. "We should check out the chocolate pastries later." His fingers tapped the table nervously. Must have been the caffeine rush after being deprived. But something felt off.

"So, Pietro, you said there was something you needed to talk to me about?" What was I doing here? Every interaction I'd had with him since the breakup had left me wanting to smash something.

"Yeah. The thing is..." It came out sounding like a question: "I wanted to apologize?"

I stared. Was this really Pietro?

"Janet, ever since we split up, my computer has worked perfectly. My kitchen appliances have made acceptable meals, and my floatcar has stopped making that funny noise." He spread his hands helplessly. "I'm bored out of my mind."

He reached for my hand, but I pulled back. Behind the counter, a dispenser started spraying iced coffee across the room.

Pietro laughed, ducking away from the stream. "I miss the way you can do that. Like that time with my food processor."

"I didn't touch the coffee dispenser. Not every malfunction that happens near me is my fault." But I couldn't help giggling at the memory of Pietro's food processor running backward, turning puree into bananas and peaches.

"How serious is this thing with your boyfriend?"

"Boyfriend?" My mind was racing. Pietro couldn't possibly know about that almost-kiss with Beau.

"I noticed at the curling match that he was wearing that necklace I gave you, only he had it as an ankle bracelet. Kind of rude, giving him a present you got from another guy."

I almost snorted whipped cream out of my nose. "I am not dating Frink. I wouldn't date any of my crew, because that would be an abuse of my position as captain." Granted, my crew didn't have much respect for my position as captain, but I figured the principle still applied. "Frink must have stolen the necklace again. He does that once in a while."

Pietro didn't seem to notice the last part. "So you're not seeing anyone?"

"Not...seriously."

"So what do you think?" His aura quivered between indigo and maroon. "About us? Getting back together?"

I took out my beepity-beeper and pulled up the post on his blog. "I'm from a disappointing species, remember? I'm too short, I'm too loud, I'm ten pounds overweight, and breaking up with me is like getting over the flu."

"I'm sorry, okay?" An impatient edge crept into his voice. My response clearly wasn't the one he'd expected. "I take it all back."

"Until next time you get mad at me. Maybe we could be friends, but..." The realization struck me as I spoke. "I've been much happier since we split up."

His voice hardened. "That Beau Dangere guy is never gonna want you."

I reached over and put my hand around Pietro's wrist. After a moment, his watch emitted a high-pitched squeal and broke into pieces.

"There. Something to remember me by." I got up. "No hard feelings; I'll pay for the coffee." I left him trying to reassemble the pieces.

11

Cheesy Mystery Novels

The trip back to Earth found me unnaturally cheerful. The rest of the crew members were all smiles with their coffee cups next to their bridge stations, and Pilar Villarreal was settled into guest quarters. Even the computer said good morning.

"It's unbelievable," I said. "Jupiter and Pluto are at peace. The people of Martia are free, and they're making enough money for all the shoes they want."

"Plus, their planet has a really cool name," Martian added.

"And you can get chocolate and coffee on any planet in the galaxy," Lola said, raising her double mocha. Her aura was gold again. It looked good on her.

Frink showed something to Nlubglub, keeping the screen turned away from me. Nlubglub stifled a high-pitched laugh.

"What?" I said.

"Nothing," they said in perfect unison.

I walked over and grabbed the communicator away from Frink. It showed the tail end of *Primarily Pietro*'s latest.

...and after I turned her down, Jam-it made my wristwatch explode, hitting the iced coffee dispenser, which went haywire and nearly injured several customers with rapid-firing ice. Note to her next boyfriend: good luck.

"That's not the funny part," Nlubglub said quickly. "Check out the comments section."

"Pietro, it's obvious you want her back. Too bad she's bound to find someone better, if she hasn't already. Because she sounds like the most badass Good Girl ever."

My heart did a tap dance. "Wow."

The beepity-beeper clangity-clunked.

"Don't answer it," everyone said simultaneously. Everyone except Zeeko.

Zeeko answered it. "Captain, it's for you."

I grimaced and took the call. "This is Captain Janet Delane."

"You have to help me. They're only allowing me one call." The viewscreen was blurry, but the voice was familiar.

"Nina Mikeljohn?"

The picture cleared up on the beepity-beeper screen. It was indeed our favorite smuggler, looking like she'd been out all night dancing in a wind tunnel. "Adequate Leader has problems with insomnia, so he reinstated the caffeine ban. Then he outlawed mystery novels because they were keeping him awake. I had to jettison a cargo hold full of police-procedural and crime-solving-dog-groomer novels before they boarded my ship."

"So if you jettisoned everything, what's the problem?"

"I was almost to the end of reading *The Dogstar of the Baskervilles*. It was right up to the scene where the detective gathered everyone in the starship's engine room to reveal the murderer, and I had to know if the robot butler did it. I tried to hide the book under my chocolate tray, but the gravity spontaneously reversed, and it flew up and smacked Richena Rossi in the face, and she arrested me."

"Richena?"

"I can't even understand how she managed to nab me. One minute her shuttlecraft was going off somewhere over the nearest moon, and the next minute she was in my shuttle bay. It's like she can be two places at once or something." A green hand gripped Nina's shoulder, presumably a Plutonian guard telling her that her time was up. "Anyway, I didn't know who to call besides you."

I glanced over at my cappuccino, just out of reach, with the foam dripping down the side. "Why would I want to go back to a planet with no coffee? Plus, I'm reading a really good suspense thriller, *Dead Body Nursery Rhyme Allusion*, and I couldn't bring it with me."

"The coffee ban made Richena Rossi pretty cranky," she said.

"How can you tell?"

"She and Beau Dangere just had a very public breakup. She caught him posting comments about you on Pietro's blog, and she had a meltdown in front of everybody, and he said he was calling off the fake engagement and requesting a transfer to a new assignment."

"We'll be right there," I said.

During the trip back to Pluto, I tried to come up with a plan. "Maybe Nlubglub could morph into a morgue cart, the rest of us will pretend to be dead bodies, and then we'll create a distraction so Frink can grab the guards' keys."

"What makes you think I can grab their keys?" Frink said.

"Because you're a convicted pickpocket?"

"Convicted means he got caught," Lola pointed out.

"He's still pretty good at swiping things," I said. "I haven't figured out where he's stashing half my socks."

"I don't have your socks!" Frink's orange eyes widened in a bad attempt at an innocent look. "That's just how the dryer is."

"Right," Martian said. "And that's not my watch underneath your sleeve?"

"Uh…"

"Never mind all that," Lola said. "The dead-body thing doesn't sound very convincing. What other distraction could we create?"

"We could pretend we're journalists for the *Galactic Times*, writing a story about the solar system's most exciting prisons," Frink suggested.

"They might have banned journalists by now," Nlubglub said. "And if they haven't, they might get around to it before we leave."

"Good point." I racked my brain. "Did they ban safety inspectors for pain-inflicting devices?"

"I have an idea." Martian turned a screen on and began sketching a device. "We bring in a small catapult that will fling a flaming mouse-trap past the guards. Then, while the guards are investigating that, we use an extendable arm to lift the keys." He added additional features to the catapult, including a snack dispenser.

"I already have extendable arms." Nlubglub demonstrated, reaching across the bridge to point at the drawing. "And how are we going to get out of there?"

"Good point: the catapult should also have the ability to tunnel through the floor. It may take me a little time to get all the parts for this."

"We don't need a new invention." Lola's aura turned a deep crimson that said she was through messing around. "Let's just start a fight. That always works."

We landed in a small docking bay near Adequate Leader's palace. I remembered that we'd gone from the ballroom to the prison section before, but I wasn't totally sure of the route. I tried asking Pilar to guide us, and she nearly choked.

"I can't go back." Despite the Plutonian cold, she started to sweat. "I nearly lost my mind in there."

"I can find it," Frink volunteered. "I usually do a little casing—I mean exploring—when I'm in a new place."

Pilar nearly fainted with relief.

The inside of the building had, if possible, grown more dank and depressing since last time we were there. Decorative black mold dripped from the corridor walls and the "Realest of the Real Planets" banners. Occasionally, there was a clean spot on the wall where a portrait of the former Exalted Leader had been removed.

Frink led us past several offices, a ballroom, and an arboretum, then stopped in front of a door. "That's either the gym or the laundry room. The quickest way is through the gym."

"I'll go in first and see if it's empty." I eased the door open. The room was dimly lit, with quiet music playing. A variety of exercise machines sat in a row, with twisted shapes to accommodate anything from tentacles to tails.

The room wasn't empty.

"Janet!" Beau sat up on one of the benches, putting down the weights he'd been lifting. In the light gravity, he could pump iron that was bigger than he was. "What are you doing here?"

I opened my mouth to tell him we were assigned to conduct book inspections to make sure all the mystery novels were gone. No, that was ridiculous. I stalled. "Why is it so dark?"

"Adequate Leader ordered all the lights dimmed to help with his insomnia." He got up and moved closer, his face flushed from the workout and his black hair slick with sweat. He'd traded his ambassadorial uniform for a t-shirt and shorts, which looked unreasonably good on him. "You have to admit, it's romantic."

"At least it makes the moldy walls look less disgusting." Ugh, I was terrible at flirting. I heard Plutonian voices in the hallway outside the door opposite the one I'd come in. I said, "Martian has something called an extreme flashlight if you want to borrow it. Only it's kind of like having a star exploding in the room."

Beau's face was setting off exploding stars in my heart. "I'm seeing a lot more clearly now. Janet, we need to talk about this thing between us. Now, while I'm away from all the drama."

The voices outside stopped right by the door. I could hear snatches of conversation, with words like "contraband" and "prison." If any Plutonians came in here, I was going to have a lot of explaining to do.

I took a step back. "This is a bad time, Beau."

"Janet, if you're not interested, just say so."

Me? He was the one who'd kept blowing me off for Richena! "It's just that I'm in the middle of this mission and—"

He touched my face. The warmth from his fingertips spread through me. "This is so much more important than any mission."

Inspiration clocked me over the head like a curling broom. "We

have a lot to talk about. Meet me in fifteen minutes outside the doors
to the prison complex."

"Prison complex?"

The far door started to open.

"There's something I need to take care of first." I ran out into the
hallway and rejoined the crew.

Frink took us through the laundry room, and I made a quick call
to Richena on the beepity-beeper. "I know everything you've been up
to. Meet me in fifteen minutes outside the prison complex."

We squeezed into the alcove outside the prison doors. It was the same
place I'd spotted Nina lifting Frink's wallet—had that really been only
a few weeks ago?

The guards had some sort of loud machinery operating inside,
helping to mask any noise. It sounded like a couple of giants snoring.

I said, "Once the fight starts, the guards should come out here to
see what's happening, and then we'll sneak in and let Nina out. Everyone ready?"

"Ready," Lola answered. "Who's fighting?"

"I've got that covered."

Beau came running up. He was early, which gave my heart a little
twinge. "Janet, can we talk now?" He noticed the crew was looking at
us. "Maybe we could go somewhere more private?"

"No, here's perfect. Almost perfect. Could we just move over
there—"

Instead he took my hands, and I forgot how to move. "I had it all
wrong," he said. "I thought I liked bad girls—the drama, the excitement. You know what? After a while, the drama isn't exciting
anymore. It's just waiting to see where the next blowup will be. But
you're not like that. You're a breath of total sanity."

"Sanity?" Martian said somewhere behind me.

"And then I saw Pietro's latest column."

I blanched. "Look, a lot of the stuff he says—"

"And then I realized you're both a good girl and a bad girl." Beau's arms slid around me. "It really is possible to have it both ways."

I didn't know what to say. And then I didn't have to say anything, because he was kissing me. I felt like I was whirling, flying through the air.

My head connected with the door, and I realized I had, in fact, been thrown through the air by an angry Richena. I cursed the low Plutonian gravity one more time.

"Have it both ways?" Richena snarled. "I'll show you both ways!"

I sat up in time to see Richena coming at me with both fists. Lola stopped her with a solid punch to the gut, and both of them tripped over Nlubglub and came crashing down on top of me. Zeeko jumped in and slugged Beau, knocking him across the room and into the opposite wall.

"Wait!" I yelled. "Zeeko, he's on our side!"

"Wait!" Martian yelled. "The fight's supposed to be over there, where the guards can see it!"

Pilar knelt next to Beau. "Could be a concussion."

Nina Mikeljohn came strolling out of the prison door. She gave an appraising look at the bodies sprawled all over the place. "What's going on?"

"We're rescuing you," Zeeko said.

"Thanks," she said, "but the guards fell asleep. Didn't you hear the snoring? They haven't adjusted well to the whole no-caffeine thing."

Beau sat up, clutching his head. "What happened?"

Richena got up and dusted herself off. Somewhere in the melee, one sleeve had gotten torn halfway off her lavender uniform. The left half of her hair had fallen out of its knot and was hanging to her shoulder. The right half was still in place. "Janet Delane attacked me."

"I what?" I tried to scramble to my feet, but I tripped over Nlubglub again.

"Don't worry," Richena told Beau. "You saved me." She tore the sleeve the rest of the way off her uniform, and knelt to wipe Beau's face with it.

"No." Beau ignored her ministrations and pulled himself up. "No, you attacked Janet. Did you think that just because I hit my head, I'd forget that you and I are split?"

Richena stood slowly, still reaching for him. "We always split up. Then we get back together."

"Not anymore." Beau turned away from her and gave me a smile that could cure the Betelgeusian Flu.

"Let's get out of here," I said. "Is everyone okay?"

A chorus of yeses responded. Nlubglub was steering Zeeko toward the exit. Frink was pocketing a pair of octagonal platinum earrings that looked suspiciously like the ones Richena had been wearing a moment ago. Martian was sketching a revised version of his catapult/drill. Lola was brushing brown mold off her uniform. Looking down, I realized my uniform was filthy as well, though not as bad as Richena's. The guards' snoring, which I'd earlier mistaken for machinery, was still audible through the doors.

"Let's get you to the infirmary and get your head examined," I told Beau.

"Now there's something I should have done a long time ago," he said.

We walked together as far as the corridor outside the infirmary, but the rest of us didn't go in, since we were technically in the middle of aiding a jailbreak. Beau leaned down to give me one more quick kiss.

A few minutes later, Lola tried to pry us apart. "Come on, we don't have all Plutonian year."

I tried to say, "I'll be right there," but it was kind of hard to talk with Beau's lips wrapped around mine. When we finally let go, my crew was down the hall and about to disappear around the corner.

"Come back soon," Beau said. He walked into the infirmary, my heart straining after him as the door closed. I pulled myself together and started after the crew.

Halfway down the hall, a door opened, and I nearly slammed into Richena. I tensed, expecting her to attack me again, but she looked at me coolly and kept walking. Her uniform was intact, her hair was perfectly coiffed in the usual knot, and she was wearing the platinum earrings that Frink had taken earlier. She passed me and went out another door.

I caught up to the crew. "Either I'm crazy, or I just saw a second Richena."

"Does it have to be one or the other?" Zeeko scrunched his forehead. "If there's a second Richena, you might still be crazy."

"A clone?" Martian pondered as we kept walking. "A hologram? Or maybe she has a tiny little planar dislocator that beams her around the city?"

I shook my head. "Her hair and makeup were fixed, so I don't think that's it, unless a planar dislocator also has hairdressing and tailoring functions."

Martian's face lit up. "That's a great idea." He pulled out a tablet and started to sketch a design.

"Not now." Lola's aura darkened. "We need to get back to the ship before Richena catches up with us, whether there's one of her or dozens."

We reached the docking port, passing rows of ships that reminded me of the parking garage that had gotten me into this whole mess. I asked Nina, "So now that you're an official convicted criminal, I suppose you'll be joining GUPPEAS?"

"Are you kidding? I'm sticking to crime. The hours are good, the pay's even better, there's no paperwork, and I don't have to wear a uniform designed by a committee." She moved closer and lowered her voice. "In fact, why don't you come work for me?"

"Be a criminal? Me?"

"You're already a criminal. How else does anyone wind up in GUPPEAS?"

"That was just a little misunderstanding over a parking space," I said.

"Criminals always get the best parking spaces."

Tempting. "Um…"

"Plus a really good supply of cheesy mystery novels for beach reading," she added.

Nlubglub turned sharply to give her a hard look, their mouth contracting into a startled O.

I said, "Isn't that what the Silver Sword was leaving for the foot-heads?"

"Martians," my brother corrected.

Nina's aqua eyes narrowed, and I once again got the impression that she was very old. Centuries old. Maybe even Jupiteran centuries.

"Nlubglub," Zeeko said suddenly, "do you speak Old Jupiteran?"

"No. Almost nobody does. Why?"

"I do," Zeeko said. "And the Old Jupiteran translation of Silver Sword is Neenyamee Quelchun." Which sounded an awful lot like Nina Mikeljohn.

Nlubglub's face stretched in disbelief. "And you didn't mention this earlier because…?"

"I don't know." Zeeko blinked his gigantic eyes. "Didn't think about it."

I was still watching Nina. "Wasn't there some legend about a 47th gender of Jupiterans, one that could impersonate other species and even eat?"

"Hey, there's my ship. Gotta go." Nina sprinted off.

12

A Piece of Asteroid From Next Week

Back on the *Turkey,* we settled in again for the flight to Earth, drinking double espressos on the bridge. "You never did tell us," Nlubglub said: "what was the story behind your being named Martian?"

"Oh, that." Martian took a slow sip of coffee, savoring the moment. Telling this story was his favorite thing in the universe. "It all started when our parents were transferred from Regulus to Saturn—see, they were in the military...."

I went back to my quarters, sent a note to my parents, and read a chapter from *The Space-Faring Moron's Guide to Common Science Fiction Plot Devices.* I was hoping it would have some advice on curling for future get-togethers with Beau, but the chapter on sports was all about various duel-to-the-death scenarios, with or without aliens wagering on them.

When I returned to the bridge, Martian was still talking. "So there was this Saturnian midwife, except you don't call it a midwife on Saturn because they're hatched instead of born. And Janet was just learning to walk back then, and somehow she climbed up to the control panel and accidentally deactivated the..."

I walked back to my quarters, steadied my nerves, and sent a message to Beau: *Do you know where your new assignment will be yet? I'll find a way to swing by there.*

I was tempted to say more, but everything between us was so new, it felt strange. I hit Send before I could embarrass myself.

I went back to the bridge, where Martian was finally winding down.

"So I was supposed to be named after my great-uncle Martin, but the midwife accidentally spelled it 'Martian,' which is the brand of Ganymedean ale she was drinking."

There was an expectant pause.

"That's it?" Nlubglub burst out. "That's the big exciting story?"

"Well, yeah," Martian said. "I think it's kind of cool."

"That's an afternoon of my centuries-long life that I'll never get back!" Nlubglub sprouted several fists just to wave them around. "It took me weeks of ritual and etymological research and meditation to come up with the name Nlubglub! And I'll bet Zeeko has a really good reason why he's named Zeeko!"

"Probably," Zeeko said, "but I was really young when I was named, so I don't remember."

"Never mind. You don't even know how to spell it." Nlubglub whirled around to face Frink. "What about you?"

"My actual name can't be pronounced in non-Ursan languages." Frink demonstrated, and the sound nearly broke the viewscreen. "It means something like *Endless ravine of orange chalcedony eternal wisdom that will last until Tuesday*, only it makes more sense in Ursan. I go by Frink because it's a Rigelian term for someone who, um, collects things."

"My name doesn't even have a story," Lola said, "and I still can't believe he wasted all that time explaining a typo!" She stomped off the bridge.

"We're getting a distress call," said a vaguely familiar voice.

I looked around. "Was that the computer?"

"Yes." Nlubglub used three fists to smack the panel. "Trying to distract us from Martian having made us sit through that."

There was a pause, as if the computer wanted to sigh but hadn't been programmed for it. "There's a distress call, and if you had a communications officer, you'd know that."

Sure enough, a barely audible distress call was fading in and out on the beepity-beeper. A shuttlecraft appeared on the viewscreen.

Then disappeared. Then appeared again.

When it disappeared a second time, Martian leaned over Frink's station. "Move the ship to these coordinates," he said. Frink began working the controls.

The *Turkey* gave a little twitch, and the distress call stopped. The computer said, "Unidentified craft has now materialized inside the shuttle bay."

I switched channels on the beepity-beeper. "This is Captain Janet Delane from GUPPEAS. You are aboard the S.S. *Turkey*. Please identify yourself."

"Janet Delane? No wonder my temporal drive stopped working," came the unmistakable voice of Richena Rossi.

I took Martian with me to the shuttle bay. We got there just in time to see Richena step out of the shuttle in a beige uniform. "Good morning, Captain," she said breezily.

I bit my tongue. "It's evening."

"Is it? It's so easy to lose track when one's using temporal technology." She strolled over to a mirrored wall panel and checked her reflection critically, tucking a hair back into her signature knot. "Hope you don't mind my hitching a ride like this."

"Once I realized it was a time-travel shuttle, I had Frink move the ship to where you were going to materialize." Martian beamed at his own cleverness.

She finally noticed Martian's presence. "You're the engineer, right? My shuttle got hit by a piece of asteroid from next week. One of the hazards of time travel. Maybe you could take a look at it."

Martian's eyes widened with something approaching ecstasy. To him, working on time-warp technology was almost as good as a planar dislocator. "I'll get my tools. Frink will want in on this too." He was out the door so fast, he might have been time-warped himself.

"Hang on," I said to Richena. "Is a time-travel shuttle even legal?"

"Define 'legal.'"

"Permissible to possess, use, or transport under the laws of the jurisdiction we're in and/or the regulations of GUPPEAS."

"They've got a committee working on a policy for it." Richena shrugged. "If they decide in favor, they'll time-warp back and make it legal retroactively. And right now we're in open space, which is no one's jurisdiction."

"That's how you wound up in GUPPEAS, isn't it? Illegal possession of a time-travel shuttle? That was what you had hidden in that storage bay."

The look she gave me could have cut the ship in half. "Beau told you that?"

"No. You just did."

Martian came barreling back in with Frink in tow and an armload of tools. They charged aboard the shuttle, whooping and squealing like children unwrapping the world's greatest birthday present. Their voices drifted out the open hatch.

"Check out the temporal drive!"

"See, the navigation system's in four dimensions—no, I think it's five."

"What does this attachment do?"

Richena glanced inside the hatch, looking amused, then turned to me. "Let me know when they're done. I have an appointment on Saturn. At least, I think I do; I misplaced my appointment book. Where are the guest quarters?"

I called Zeeko on the beepity-beeper and asked him to come here and escort her. I needed to get away from Richena before my head turned into a volcano.

As the door shut behind me, the last thing I heard was Martian's voice from the hatch: "She's going to notice if you steal that."

I walked in the direction away from the guest quarters, which led me down a dead-end hallway to the first officer's quarters. I knocked and Lola answered, looking surprised.

"Technically you're not supposed to be here," she said. "The first officer's quarters are always at the opposite end of the ship from the captain, so that if a giant space squid or anything takes a bite out of one end of the ship, the crew will still have one person to lead them in the fight against it."

"Until the squid takes a second bite?"

"Well, yes. Obviously." She let me in.

The room was an overwhelming attack of pink. Pink walls, pink bedspread, pink meditation crystal, and some wicked-looking pink plants. The different shades matched her usual aura colors. A pair of antique battle axes hung on the wall. There were some paper books on the shelf, one of which was entitled *1000 Ways to Get Away With Murder.*

I said, "Didn't I see that book in Frink's quarters?"

"Probably. I have to get my stuff back from him on a regular basis."

"And you have this book because…?"

"Strictly as a precaution, of course. In case I ever need it." Her aura brightened. "Why, did you decide to finally get rid of Zeeko?"

"Uh, no. We're in a peace organization." I was pretty sure she was kidding, but I didn't want to push it. "We have a small problem, for which I'm sure there's a peaceful solution." I explained about Richena's sudden arrival and the time-travel shuttle.

"A time-travel shuttle." She poured us coffee, thinking. "That's what she had in the closed-off storage bay. That's why she always seemed to be a step ahead of us."

"Until it broke down. But now we're taking her back to Earth with it. It'll get confiscated, and she'll be arrested, and…well, actually, she'll probably just have to spend more time in GUPPEAS."

"You're enjoying the thought of making her look bad, aren't you?"

"Maybe." I took the pink coffee cup she offered.

"You and Beau should fix up your exes. Pietro could write blog posts about Richena's time travels, and she could design him a better wardrobe."

"I'm not letting Richena get me down, or Pietro either." I got up, feeling energized. "Beau's with me, we made peace with Pluto, we worked out a treaty with a new planet, we have a fuelstone source that isn't constantly in the middle of a war, and the crew's getting good at curling. Maybe things are finally working out."

"Sure," Lola said, blowing on her extra-hot coffee. "What could possibly go wrong?"

On my way back to my quarters, I stopped back at the shuttle bay. Martian and Frink were still gleefully working on the engine. I told them, "After you finish, seal the shuttle door shut."

"Is that really necessary?" Richena's voice behind me lowered my body temperature by a couple of degrees.

I turned. "Thought you were in guest quarters."

"Your crew member seems to be taking his time getting here. You want to seal the shuttle because…?"

"GUPPEAS hasn't made a decision yet on whether it's legal."

Richena smirked. "Always the good girl, going by the book."

Zeeko wandered in. "Sorry, I forgot the shuttle bay got moved to this side of the ship after the accident. Wait, that was before you were here, Captain. Sort of."

I had no idea what he was talking about, but I didn't want to admit that in front of Richena. "You know the way to guest quarters, right?"

"Sure, it's just past that giant splotch on the wall shaped like a Uranian lava-beetle." He headed for the door.

Richena gave me a smug look that bothered me long after they were out of sight.

In the morning, I had a bad feeling pressing on me like moisture in the air. Maybe it was just from the new motivational poster, which showed a glowing box with the words: *Think outside the box. What's inside might be radioactive.*

I checked my beepity-beeper and found two notifications—and one of them was a reply from Beau. My bad mood melted into excitement. I pulled up the message.

Dear Captain Delane: I didn't understand your question about a new assignment. I'm on Pluto for the foreseeable future. What was it you wanted to meet about?—Amb. Beau Dangere.

I stared at the screen. What in the twenty-nine multiverses was this? It didn't sound like Beau at all. It was as if the last few days hadn't happened.

I finally remembered to check the second notification, which sent me running to the bridge to confront Frink. "What did you steal out of Richena's shuttle?"

"What? Nothing."

The crew busied themselves at their stations, trying to pretend they weren't watching my fuming.

"The seal was overridden at 2200 hours last night."

"Wasn't me." Frink looked genuinely surprised. "I can prove it. I was stealing Nlubglub's favorite chair. It's in my quarters."

Nlubglub looked up. "What?"

Zeeko scrunched his forehead. "But with time travel, couldn't he have been both places?"

"GUPPEAS port of entry just gave us permission to land on Earth," Frink said. "Initiating landing sequence."

We landed in the GUPPEAS dock, and I was gratified to see the crowd assembled to greet us, standing at attention in dress uniforms, looking like a rainbow that had been carved up with a chainsaw. One side of the room held an impressive buffet that contained no dried regelworm whatsoever. On the other side of the room was a brass band playing some country song. It might have been "You've Made the Down Payment but You Haven't Signed the Mortgage on My Heart."

As we stepped off the ship, a cheer went up from the crowd. I glimpsed a banner hanging over us: CONGRATULATIONS, CAPTAIN!

Cameras flashed, and I spotted Pietro's aura among the reporters. The GUPPEAS Steering Committee walked right up to me...and right past...and surrounded Richena. Vertin Bogler announced, "On behalf of the Galactic Universal Peacemongering Paradigm Emergent Action Spacefleet, our congratulations to Captain Richena Rossi for freeing the citizens of the planet Martia, opening up the fuelstone market, and paving the way for peace between Jupiter and Pluto!"

"Wait a minute!" I yelled, but my voice was drowned out by cheers around us. My bewildered crew all started talking at once. Might as well have been trying to make ourselves heard in the middle of mortal combat between two planet-sized pachyderms.

Someone from the Steering Committee took the microphone. "Captain Rossi also saved a prominent member of our community, Dr. Pilar Villarreal." A stunned-looking Pilar was picked up, hoisted onto the shoulders of the Steering Committee, and carried off. They took her somewhere near the stage, and I lost sight of her.

Bogler went on, "We are honored to present this Medal of Distinguished Service to Captain Rossi. In fact, since this is the first one we've ever given, we've decided to call it the Rossi Award. Its shape is in honor of the nickname Captain Rossi was known by during her brave acts on Martia: a silver sword."

"What?" I sputtered. "She's not the Silver Sword!" The cheers were deafening, and no one heard me.

Richena glanced over at me and gave a slow, malicious smile.

I elbowed my way through the crowd until I was next to Bogler. "I really need to talk to you."

"Captain Delane, this isn't the time—"

I pulled him into the hallway with my crew following. "I don't think you understand what really happened with Captain Rossi. Like with the Martians, and the fuelstone, it was actually my crew—"

"Captain, I was starting to say this isn't the best time to deal with unpleasant subjects, at a gathering to honor Captain Rossi." His aura turned an unsettling shade of lima-bean green. "But we've been informed that there's an illegal time-travel shuttle aboard your ship."

"Yes, about that—"

"So you admit you have it?"

"Richena Rossi brought it aboard. The ship's logs will show it."

But the ship's logs wouldn't show anything of the sort, I realized slowly. Because after she'd had my crew fix the shuttle, Richena had broken the seal, gone back in time, and made a few changes. I was doomed.

"Also, I went back through the records for your ship, and it looks like there was a mistake made in assigning you as captain. The captain of your ship was supposed to be someone named"—he looked it up on his beepity-beeper—"Plutherxib."

"Who?"

"Not sure of the pronunciation. It's spelled P-L-U-T-H-E-R-X-I-B."

Looks of horror plastered across an assortment of faces, as my crew and I realized that was how Zeeko spelled his name.

"Never heard of them," Lola, Frink, Nlubglub, Martian, and I all said simultaneously.

"I suppose we'll have to keep you on, then," Bogler said.

Zeeko just kept smiling.

Across the room, a bewildered Pilar was being photographed with Richena underneath the welcome banner. Richena took the microphone. "I'd like to thank Secretary Bogler and all of the GUPPEAS leadership, Pluto's Adequate Leader, and of course the love of my life, without whom none of this would be possible: Ambassador Beau Dangere. My fiancé."

Beau emerged from the crowd and embraced Richena, his face glowing with pride. Of course, I realized with a pang: she'd changed that too, when she went back in time. They were back together, or they'd never broken up.

Beau glanced my way, and just for a moment his face clouded with confusion.

Richena went on with her speech, thanking pretty much everyone in the galaxy except my crew. She was still wearing that evil smile. If I'd had an actual silver sword, I had a pretty good idea of where I'd have liked to stick it right then.

"Peace organization," I reminded myself under my breath. "Peace. Peace."

13

A Town Still Not Called Martian

My only hope of avoiding punishment for having the shuttle was to argue GUPPEAS into making time-travel devices legal aboard GUPPEAS ships. Which required me to attend a committee meeting, with my item as the 97th piece of business. After getting lost a couple of times in the headquarters, I arrived at a room full of disgruntled humans, even-less-gruntled aliens, and a box of crumbly rocks that might have started off as donuts.

"Is this the meeting for the GUPPEAS Directional Committee?" I asked.

A Saturnian swiveled her eyestalks toward me. "This is the pre-meeting meeting."

"The what?"

"Where we set the agenda and prioritize," a weary Venusian man explained, his aura dimming by the moment. He glared at a chair until I sat down.

I leaned over to the Earthling next to me and whispered, "How does this work?"

"Work?" she answered drily. She was taking rapid notes, and she already had an encyclopedia-sized pile of papers in front of her.

Some sort of large bird was speaking now. "We need a vision statement, a mission statement, and a snappier logo."

"And a new name," squeaked a tiny Betelgeusian. "Something like The Universal—Or Multiversal If There Are Multiple Universes—

Paradigmatic Fleet of Space-Traveling Persons Who Monger Peace."

"Only snappier," added the bird.

If only the Plutonians had taken me prisoner, I thought helplessly. *I could be in a nice dungeon right now, being tortured with dental drills or something.*

"After we deal with time-travel rules, any chance we could talk about changing the uniforms?" I asked. "Maybe have them be just one color?" It was the last time I got a word in for the next twelve hours.

"Janet, wake up!"

"Nooo." I was having a lovely dream in which I went back to work at the edible-air factory, except it had been converted to a chocolate factory, I worked in quality control, and a gorgeous interstellar ambassador wanted to be my boyfriend.

"Janet!" Martian was shaking me awake.

I yawned and opened my eyes. I was slumped over the conference table at the meeting room, my head resting on the donut box. "Is the meeting over? Did they decide about the shuttle? What about the uniforms?" I picked up a document someone had left behind, which turned out to be the proposed new name for GUPPEAS, all six pages of it.

"They adjourned without a decision, but that's not important right now. Pluto's at war with Jupiter."

"No, it isn't. We fixed all that, remember?" I brushed donut crumbs off my cheek.

"They started it up again," he said. "Nlubglub was at the table tennis championship, and there was a Plutonian woman in the audience, and she called Nlubglub 'him' instead of 'them,' and Nlubglub called her mother a three-legged space worm and said she hadn't changed socks in seven Plutonian years. Then Nlubglub chased her back to her ship, and she flew over to Jupiter and started shooting, and they shot back." Martian took a breath. "Nobody's actually hit anything yet, and the shields should last another 300 years or so."

I let this sink in. "Nlubglub restarted the war with Pluto?"

"Pretty much, yeah."

"What the hell is a three-legged space worm?"

"I don't know," he said. "I'm not sure if there is such a thing, but it sounded bad."

I rattled the crumbs in the donut box in the futile hope that there would be something edible left. "Remind me, how hard is it to kill a Jupiteran?"

"You can't kill your own crew members. There's some kind of regulation against it."

"Are you sure?" I stared at the pile of paper in front of me. "I could probably sneak in a rule change at one of these meetings."

I followed Martian back to the *Turkey,* still docked outside GUPPEAS headquarters. On the bridge, a sheepish-looking Nlubglub said, "Captain, there's a—"

"Shut up. I'm not talking to you. What kind of security chief starts a war?"

"I was just going to tell you there's a message from the Under-secretary to the Oversecretary." Nlubglub pointed to the computer panel, then retreated to the far corner of the bridge, trying to blend in with the equipment.

I played back the message. Vertin Bogler's smarmy face and lime-green aura filled the computer screen. "Captain Delane, everyone was impressed with your suggestion to redesign the uniforms. We've decided to model the new ones on Captain Rossi's designs." Not entirely bad news, I decided. She might be a man-stealing, glory-hogging drama queen, but she had great taste. Bogler held up a sample. "Here's the redesigned logo that will appear on every uniform." The letters G-U-P-P-E-A-S formed a caricature of Richena's face, complete with the knot of hair on top of her head.

The recording switched off. I could have sworn the image of Richena lingered for a moment after Bogler's face disappeared.

"That's it." I kicked the computer panel, setting off a shower of sparks. "That's the particle that broke the particle converter's back."

Zeeko gave me a bland look. "The particle converter's broken?"

"No," I said, "I mean that's the last straw. In the past year I've been arrested, dumped, ridiculed, caffeine-deprived, put in charge of a ship full of lunatics, shot at, threatened, semi-bludgeoned, marooned, and used as a stone in a curling match. I had to protect a planet from chocolate. Do you hear me? Chocolate!"

"It sounds bad when you put it that way," Zeeko admitted, "but this ship isn't actually *full* of lunatics. There's only six of us, and that's counting you."

"Seven if there's a Plutonian saboteur," Lola added.

This wasn't helping. I got up. "I am going to undo every worthless minute of this last year. I am going to make it un-happen."

Nlubglub morphed back into their normal shape and gave me an alarmed look, or what passed for an alarmed look on a giant purple rubber ball. "Captain, you're not thinking about taking that shuttle."

Of course I was. It was too perfect: a shuttle with time-travel capability, right when we were docked in New Saint Harmony York Springs. I stormed down the hallway from the bridge to the shuttle bay, with the rest of the crew scurrying after me as I ranted. "I want my life back. I want back every minute that I've spent in this insane bureaucratic hell. And while I'm at it, maybe I can get them to name the town Nerthus or something."

"Or Martian," Martian added hopefully.

"You have a whole species named after you," I snapped. "Don't get greedy. Nerthus is a cooler name anyway. It's a Danish earth goddess, and it's fun to say."

It fell to Frink, of all people, to advise me against theft. "Captain, you can't take the shuttle. The Temporal Technology Committee finally made a decision, and they're keeping the ban on time travel. They're going to use remote control to remove it from the ship. If you get caught taking the shuttlecraft, they'll send you to prison."

"Yes, but once I fix the past, then I won't have taken it, because I won't be here and this whole mess will never have happened."

As we entered the shuttle bay, something inside the shuttle started to click and whir softly.

"Didn't you read *The Space-Faring Moron's Guide to Common Science Fiction Plot Devices*?" Nlubglub argued. "Time-travel paradoxes never work out the way you think they will. What if you overshoot it, go back to before you were born, and cause your parents never to meet? You'd never exist at all."

"Then I can't go to prison for stealing the shuttle, can I?"

"Wait," Martian said. "Would I still exist?"

The whirring noise got louder. The shuttle rose slowly, just a few inches off the ground.

"I'm not going back that far," I said. "I'm going back a few months and getting us both out of this ridiculous organization."

"Oh, let her do it," Lola said wearily. "Maybe our next captain will actually have some idea how to run a ship."

Zeeko took a moment to consider this. "No, probably not."

Lights came on inside the shuttle. It was going to phase out soon. I had one chance.

Nlubglub moved between me and the shuttle door. "Captain, if you take one more step, I'll have to arrest you." They sprouted a pair of arms and reached toward me.

I picked up Nlubglub and threw them straight into Frink's stomach. Frink fell back onto Zeeko, who fell onto Martian. Lola stepped aside and watched the whole fiasco with disdain, straightening her uniform sash as her aura turned a toxic pink.

"The manual override is the third knob from the left," she said.

I yanked the door open, hurled myself into the shuttle, and slammed the door behind me. My heart raced to the pit of my stomach and started busily churning my breakfast.

I sat down at the console. Which one had Lola said was for overriding the autopilot? There were twice as many dials and knobs as I was used to, with one meter counting down and another counting up. Where was Frink when I needed him? Oh yeah—outside with a flattened Jupiteran on top of him.

I found the timer and set it for the day of the town hall meeting, the day I'd left my drab but reasonably sane life and become the captain of a ship that still didn't have a real name. Enough already. Turn back time, and turkey would be nothing more than a flavor of tofu that Martian cooked on holidays.

The shuttle vibrated and winked out of existence.

Then it winked back into existence and crashed through the side of the ship.

I had just enough time to look back and see the gaping hole I'd left in the *Turkey.* First Zeeko, then Martian, then the whole crew stared out after me. *At least I didn't do this while we were in space,* I thought. Then everything went dark again.

The shuttle materialized in the parking garage, next to a column of tightly packed floatcars. My old one was sitting a couple of rows up, its distinctive intersecting-canoes shape impossible to miss. This had to be the right night. I could hear the loudspeakers across the street as people babbled on about naming the town. I couldn't resist scanning the crowd until I saw myself staring back. I grinned and waved, although of course she/I couldn't see me through the opaque view-screen on the shuttle. My old self had no idea what I was saving us from tonight. I maneuvered the time-travel shuttle over to a parking spot just below a folded-up floatcar, and hit the controls to deactivate.

"Unauthorized access," the computer intoned. The shuttle vibrated with a high-pitched hum. "Initiating self-destruct sequence in sixty seconds. Fifty-nine. Fifty-eight."

"What? No. Abort. Abort!" I shoved my captain's insignia against the control panel. "Authorization, Captain Janet Delane."

The countdown stopped, but the vibration continued. "Stand by for security question." The instrument panel was already heating up.

The next few seconds felt like a Plutonian year.

The computer said, "In science fiction, what is the surest sign that one is living in a dystopia?"

How in the universe was I supposed to know? Of all the questions Richena could have picked for—

Wait. I knew this one. It was in *The Space-Faring Moron's Guide to Common Science Fiction Plot Devices.* "Paperwork."

"Canceling self-destruct sequence."

The humming stopped, and the temperature eased its way down. Unbelievable: a computer had listened to me. Maybe I was finally over my technology hex?

The shuttlecraft rattled back and forth.

I could see what was coming, and there was no way to stop it. The shuttle hit the folded-up floatcar above me, which unfolded to its full size and slammed into my old floatcar. My past self and I watched in unison as the bulky old floatcar streaked across the sky and buried itself in the roof of the town hall. Ever so slightly to the left of the place where it had hit before.

Two burly Alpha Centaurian guards started toward the garage. I had no idea what would happen if both of me got arrested. Would we have to serve simultaneous sentences in GUPPEAS?

The loudspeaker boomed, "Janet—"

I frantically hit buttons on the shuttle, blasting back to my own time. Maybe no one would know I'd been there.

When I reached the dock, I found the *Turkey.* But the hole in the side was gone. I looked down at the controls, trying to make sense of the readings. Where—no, *when* was I? Both chronometers were jumping around, not stopping long enough for me to get a reading. I tried to adjust them, forgetting to look at the navigation instruments.

The shuttle crashed through the tail of the ship, and skidded to a stop in the shuttle bay. A lone crew member turned and looked with mild curiosity. Zeeko.

I opened the hatch and popped my head out. "Excuse me, I think there's been some sort of mistake. Could you tell me the date?"

"I don't remember." Zeeko looked it up on his beepity-beeper and showed me. "Here it is."

The same day as my floatcar accident. I'd moved in space but not time. The damage I'd seen on my first day as captain was my own doing. "One more question. Do you know which control is the manual override on a time-travel shuttle?"

"Third from the left. Are you the new captain?"

"Yes, but not yet. Probably best not to mention this to me when I come back."

He shrugged. "Okay."

I found the right knob and blasted off again.

I returned to the right time, but the crew barely noticed when I maneuvered the shuttle back into place on the ship. They were gathered around a spot where I'd ripped open the hull on my way out. I emerged from the shuttle and found them crowded together with their backs to me, chattering and pointing. I squeezed past Martian and Nlubglub.

In between the torn metal walls, a narrow hidden passageway had been exposed. Inside stood the scrawniest, saddest-looking Plutonian I've ever seen, wearing a robe made from stitched-together socks.

I looked him up and down. "You're the Plutonian saboteur?"

"I'm not a saboteur," he said. "That thing with the semi-explosion in the engine room was totally an accident. And I had nothing to do with the last time a shuttle blasted a hole in the ship wall—that was the previous captain, or something."

"You've sabotaged my wardrobe," Frink said, lifting his pant legs to show mismatched socks. He seemed genuinely miffed that someone else on the ship was stealing. "I don't think I have a single pair of socks left."

"But the robe looks good, don't you think?" the Plutonian said. "I'm going to make a matching hat next."

I wasn't sure how to define "matching" when the socks in question were argyle silk, green wool, lavender cotton, polka-dotted corduroy, and red fishnet, patchworked together in no particular order. "I want my coffee-injecting alarm clock back. And if you're not a saboteur, who are you and what are you doing on my ship?"

"My name's Skeeder Boredan. I got kicked off of Pluto a few months ago for sleeping through an anti-Jupiter rally."

"A criminal, eh?" I said. "We could probably get you enlisted in GUPPEAS."

He brightened. "Really?"

Two Alpha Centaurian security guards marched onto the ship, looking remarkably like the ones I'd just seen at the town hall meeting. "Captain Janet Delane? We have orders to arrest you for illegal use of time-travel technology, and wanton and aesthetically displeasing damage to your ship."

"Hang on a second," I said, then turned back to my crew. "That other captain you had before me, who took the shuttle and knocked a hole in the ship? That was me, right?"

"Yes," Zeeko said. "But you told me not to mention it to you."

Lola tried to smack him and missed. "Why didn't you tell the rest of us?"

He shrugged. "Didn't think about it."

My brain was rattling like the shuttle had earlier. "How many timelines are there? Is there one where Beau and I wind up together?" I had more questions, but the security guards were dragging me away.

The next few hours left me sitting in a cell, waiting for my hearing. The room was obnoxiously sterile, except for one wall where various former inhabitants had scratched out their names. Frink's name reappeared several times. With nothing else to do, I finished reading *The Space-Faring Moron's Guide to Common Science Fiction Plot Devices*. The section on time travel wasn't terribly helpful.

Use of time travel to solve one problem invariably creates another, or recreates the same problem. Otherwise, there would be no tension in the plot, since all problems including one's own gruesome and untimely death by paper cuts could be fixed by the convenient insertion of a time-travel do-over.

The door slid open, and a couple of guards tossed Pilar Villarreal inside, then shut the door again. "What are you doing here?" I asked. "And why do you smell like chocolate?"

"Don't want to talk about it." She curled up in the corner, staring at the names on the wall. "It's already gotten four million views on social media."

I discreetly took out my beepity-beeper and typed *Pilar Villarreal arrest.* The footage came up immediately. It started with the image of a banquet table laid out with roast finfin and brightly colored fruits. In the center was a multi-tiered display of cupcakes, alternating chocolate and vanilla, arranged to resemble a wedding cake.

The view widened to show the party guests at tables, and Richena canoodling with Beau. Richena was in an elegant black dress and pearls. She rose to address the gathering.

"Thank you all for coming to our engagement party. The gift table is over there, by the fish tank. Beau and I were brought so much closer by our time on Pluto, where I was working undercover as the Silver Sword."

"You are not the Silver Sword!"

The camera swung to show Pilar storming up to Richena. "You only invited me to this party for the publicity, hoping I'd go along with your story about you being the hero. The Silver Sword is a Jupiteran chocolate smuggler, and the real hero was Janet Del—"

Richena shoved a cupcake into Pilar's mouth.

Pilar grabbed the top tier of cupcakes and crammed it in Richena's face.

They erupted into an all-out cupcake battle, with pastries flying everywhere. Beau tried to get in between and separate them. Moments later, guards dragged Pilar and Richena away.

The clip ended, and I glanced over at Pilar. "Richena's in the next cell," she said. "Looks like I'm getting drafted into GUPPEAS."

"How would you feel about being chief medical officer on the *Turkey*?"

The door opened again, and Martian bounded into the room before we were shut in again. "Oh no," I said, "not you too. Are they arresting the whole crew?"

"What? No, nothing like that." He looked around, like he'd forgotten he was in jail. "I just couldn't wait to tell you, so I remote-programmed the guards' weapons to slap them so they'd arrest me."

"You couldn't wait to tell me what?" From the look of him, it had to be good news. Jupiter and Pluto had made peace again? Richena Rossi had fallen into a black hole? This whole brain-deprived GUPPEAS bureaucracy had been disbanded and we were going home?

He sat down next to me, grinning. "Janet, I checked my gravy mixer, and it turns out I forgot to take out one of the frog-cloning components. Do you realize what this means?"

I didn't. "Another really messy Thanksgiving?"

"It means you don't have a technology hex. You never did. It was me that messed up the gravy mixer. The engine explosion was the Plutonian stowaway. Zeeko bumped the planar dislocator. Richena Rossi's electronic datebook was working perfectly; we just didn't realize she was using time travel to keep two appointments at the same time. And I'll bet you anything Nina Mikeljohn sabotaged the equipment at the fuelstone factory when it almost fell on us."

"Really?" For some reason, this made me feel better. I leaned against the door, feeling electricity hum through the automatic locking mechanism.

The power went out.

"I got nothing," Martian's voice said in the darkness.

It took the guards three hours to manually cut the cell door off with a blowtorch. We all wound up in front of the robot magistrate, along with the Plutonian stowaway in his robe of stitched-together socks.

"Skeeder Boredan," the robot intoned, "you are found guilty of illegal entry on a GUPPEAS ship, along with maliciously negligent sabotage of the engine and hosiery larceny."

The Plutonian was grinning broadly. "So I get to join GUPPEAS?"

"Yes. You are hereby assigned to Captain Rossi's ship, and also to the committee to re-redesign the uniforms."

"Thank you! Thank you!" Skeeder Boredan all but skipped over to Richena, who was sitting in the back with Beau. Richena looked over his sock robe with undisguised horror.

Pilar got sentenced to a year in GUPPEAS, and Richena and Martian both had their assignments extended. Finally, it was my turn.

"Captain Janet Delane, you are charged with possession of an illegal time-travel shuttlecraft, and involuntary malicious renovation of both your ship and the Janet City Hall."

"But I—Wait, the what city hall?"

"City Hall," it repeated. "For the City of Janet."

"They named it Janet? How did I do that?" I'd changed history after all. Sure, the town hall was still a smoking mess—but it was a smoking mess with a cool name.

"Yes, the owner of the floatcar had the same name as you. Funny that." The robot's monotone didn't change when it used the word *funny.* "When they tried to order her to report to security, the loudspeaker said 'Janet' and then fizzled out. So everyone thought that was the new name."

"Because the floatcar hit a little to the left this time." My head was spinning. "The City of Janet. That's fun to say." And every time Pietro or Richena mentioned the town where GUPPEAS was headquartered, they'd have to say my name.

"Your choices are prison, the military, or another year in the Galactic Universal Peacemongering Paradigm Emergent Action Spacefleet."

I looked over at my crew, all sitting in the front row. Zeeko was watching a video of dancing lizards, Frink had his hand in somebody's purse, Nlubglub was glaring at a Plutonian across the room, Pilar was sneaking a chocolate chip cookie, and Lola was doing her nails in a poisonous shade of blood red.

"Prison," I said firmly.

The court clerk checked his computer. "No can do. There's a power outage, and we can't unlock any of the cells right now."

"You can't stop sending people to prison," I argued. "What if I killed somebody? You'd put me back in the peace force?"

"No," the robot said wearily, "we'd rent out a prison on another planet and charge you 44 million credits for transport. Why, were you planning to kill somebody? It's almost lunchtime, so make a decision. GUPPEAS or no?"

I looked at the crew again. Zeeko was excitedly showing Martian his video, with the lizards doing the big dance number at the end of Queelchu's movie *There Is No Hurling in Curling*.

The robot added, "Otherwise we'll have to find a new captain for the next mission of escorting Ambassador Dangere to the Orion Nebula."

I turned and looked straight at Beau. He looked at me like he was trying to catch a memory fluttering just out of his reach.

I told the judge, "Put me back on the *Turkey.*"

"The what?"

"My ship. It doesn't have an official name."

"Actually, it does," the court clerk said. "It was registered this morning as the *Cosmic Old York Nerthus Turkey.*"

"Close enough," I said.

TIMELESS BOOKS • QUALITY AUTHORS

www.ThinklingsBooks.com
Facebook.com/ThinklingsBooks
@ThinklingsBooks

Thinklings Books started out when three speculative-fiction-loving professional editors—Jeannie Ingraham, Deborah Natelson, and Sarah Awa—got together and formed a writing group. We called ourselves the Thinklings, in honor of C.S. Lewis and J.R.R. Tolkien's group, the Inklings.

Over time, we found ourselves agonizing more and more about how messed-up the publishing industry had become. Why couldn't good books get published? Why were so many bad books published just because their authors had big Twitter followings? We wished there were something we could do about the problem . . . and then we realized there was.

As a developmental editor, a substantive/line editor, and a proofreader, the three of us knew good writing when we saw it—and we knew how to make it even better. We had a lot of experience walking our clients through the publishing process—both traditional and self-publish—and we had contacts with marketing and design experts. We had some amazing unpublished books lined up and ready for production. We had, in fact, everything we needed to make a great publishing company. All that was left was to actually do it.

So we're doing it.

Spectacular Reads. Every Time.

I will win.

The plan was to keep my head down, do my job, bring endless rounds of coffee to my genius boss. But see, I have this thing about bullies. Doesn't matter who they are—evil fairies, ravenous demons, powerful traitors, or my own family. The moment they try to enslave my brothers, murder my king, and fold up my boss like a literal hand towel, they're my enemies.

I don't have magic. I don't have power. I don't even have much money. But as long as I have a brain and a will, there's nothing I won't do to save the people and the country I love.

So bring it on.

Bargaining Power by Deborah J. Natelson

One bite on her hand…a million problems
slipping through her fingers.

After a wild animal attack, Melanie Caldwell thinks she just needs to go to the doctor. Then she's kidnapped on the day of the next full moon, and discovers in the worst way that monsters are real…and that she has become one of them.

All Melanie wanted was to get a boyfriend and graduate college. Now she has to deal with agonizing monthly transformations, a secret organization stalking her, friends and enemies trying to discover her secret, and hunters looming on the horizon.

Hunter's Moon by Sarah M. Awa

The Narrative Must Be Obeyed

Everyone in the Taskmaster's Realm knows how the story goes: the boy of destiny goes on a quest, defeats the dark lord, and gets the swooning princess. It's a great story, if you happen to be a knight or a wizard or a hero. But it's pretty odious if you're Ordinary: a barmaid who has to inflate her bosom and have her backside pinched, a homely prince who can't buckle his swash because his face doesn't fit, or a soldier who gets killed over and over and over again just to progress the plot.

Fodder of Humble Village is one of those soldiers, and, frankly, he's sick and tired of getting speared, decapitated, and disembowelled so the good guys can look glorious. In fact, he's not going to take it anymore.

No matter what The Narrative tries to make him do.

The Disposable by Katherine Vick

Immeasurable imagination. Unmitigated magic.
Spectacular style.

The clockwork man is crafted, to begin with—commissioned by that terrible tyrant Time to serve as her slave for all eternity. His brain boasts balance wheels and torsion springs; he can wind himself up with a key in his side; and, most importantly, his gyroscopic tourbillon heart glimmers with pure diamond.

He is a living being and he is art, and he refuses to remain a slave forever. He therefore slips through Time's fingers as the Sands of Time slip through the cracks of reality (at least, when the time cats aren't using them as a litter box).

Among astounding adventures, despite harrowing hardships, and in between escaping interfering enchanters, the clockwork man seeks his imagination, his purpose, and his name.

The Land of the Purple Ring by Deborah J. Natelson

Beware of Spilling Ink

Skate is a thief, trained and owned by the local crime syndicate, the Ink. When she tries to burgle a shut-in's home, she gets caught by the owner—a powerful undead wizard. He makes a deal with her: "borrow" books from other wizards in return for a place to stay.

Caught between her growing fondness for the wizard and her past with the crime syndicate, Skate doesn't know where her loyalties lie. But she'd better figure it out, because there's a new player in town, one whose magical hypnotism puts them all at risk.

Skate the Thief by Jeff Ayers

True Love vs. Ancient Curses

When the Egyptology department needs funds to offset a recent spate of museum thefts, Theodora Speer grudgingly trades her painting smock for an evening gown. Charming donors isn't usually her idea of a good time—but then, she doesn't usually get to meet handsome and mysterious men like Seth Adler.

Seth Adler is desperate to get close to a very specific Egyptian mummy, and attending a fundraising gala seems just the ticket. He doesn't expect to meet Theo, refreshing in her honesty and intriguing him against his will . . . and he definitely doesn't expect her to interfere with his plans.

Frantic to escape before the police catch up, Seth kills himself in front of Theo. Except it turns out he's not so dead after all, and it's up to Theo to keep him that way. Even if it means fleeing the police, practicing ancient Egyptian magic, and confronting the real thief.

Painter of the Dead by Catherine Butzen

About the Author

Laura Ruth Loomis is a social worker by day, space cadet by night. She writes contemporary fiction as well as science fiction and fantasy. Her contemporary chapbook of linked short stories, *Lost in Translation*, is available from Wordrunner Press. Her fiction and nonfiction have appeared in *Writer's Digest, On the Premises, Prime Number, Women on Writing*, and elsewhere.

The Cosmic Turkey had its genesis in middle school, when Laura would write stories to keep herself entertained. Decades later, when she was stuck on other writing projects, she thought back to a time when writing was pure fun, and the *Turkey* flew once more.

Laura lives in Northern California, with her wife Terry, their assorted pets, and possibly a Plutonian saboteur who keeps stealing their socks.

Acknowledgements

There have been so many writers, readers, critique partners, and editors who helped me along the way. Thanks especially to Aline Soules (curling consultant), Alvin Greenberg, Chris Lavin, Dean Gloster, Deborah Jeanne Natelson and Sarah Awa (editors extraordinaire), Dennis Cusack, Dirk von der Horst, Edward Van Winkle, Gloria Lenhart, Jack Champlin, Karen Schwabach, Kenya Aissa, Laura Remington, Lenka Glassner, Melissa Welter, Sara Adams, T. K. Barber, the Alameda Wordsmiths, and the Oberon Creative Writing Club.

Eddie Vela, may you find peace among the stars.

Special thanks to Stephanie Carr, a writer who makes amazing things seem effortless, and who has never been wrong when she says, "This scene needs more punch."

Thanks to my parents, Jim and Mary Loomis, for your unwavering faith, encouragement, and tolerance for nonsense. And to my brother, Patrick Loomis, the original Martian. And to my niece, Jennifer Marshall, my favorite target audience.

First, last, and always, thanks to my wife, Terry Silva. You make every story into happily-ever-after.